MW01136035

IT'S CRAZY
TO STAY CHINESE
IN MINNESOTA

1017-TELE

IT'S CRAZY TO STAY CHINESE IN MINNESOTA

Chasing Bingo Tang

Eleanor Wong Telemaque

017-TELE

Copyright © 2000 by Eleanor Wong Telemaque

Library of Congress Number: 00-190329
ISBN #:   Hardcover   0-7388-1730-9
              Softcover   0-7388-1731-7

Cover Design By Jeanette Wong Ming

All rights reserved. No part of this book may be reproduced or transmitted in any form or by any means, electronic or mechanical, including photocopying, recording, or by any information storage and retrieval system, without permission in writing from the copyright owner.

This is a work of fiction. Names, characters, places and incidents either are the product of the author's imagination or are used fictitiously, and any resemblance to any actual persons, living or dead, events, or locales is entirely coincidental.

This book was printed in the United States of America.
To order additional copies of this book, contact:
Xlibris Corporation
1-888-7-XLIBRIS
www.Xlibris.com
Orders@Xlibris.com

CONTENTS

To Ruby & Huey, Michael & Janice, Terry & Grace, Bruce,
Rod, Gloria & Ed, Jock, Don, Vicky, Madeline, Jody, Andy,
Jeanette, Eric, Johnny, Anita, Jennifer, Sherry & John, Nancy
and especially to Ady and Maury
and to Love.

Also to Dr. Fritz Telemaque who made this
second edition possible;
and to his children.

CHAPTER ONE

As long ago as I can remember, my Chinese mother said: "If you have a rice shop, you can send money back to China."

As long as I can remember, my Chinese father said: "If you have a rice shop, you can go to college and become a pharmacist."

I figured that's why I grew up in a Chinese restaurant in the Middle West. It was in a small town on the Iowa-Minnesota border.

Called the Canton, the restaurant was owned by my father and Uncle Fung. It was kind of a bastard Chinese restaurant, where they served roast milk-fed turkey along with the usual *chop suey* and *chow mein*.

In those years the Chinese in Minnesota were trying to better themselves, either by owning shares in a restaurant or by running gambling parlors. Partly because of discrimination, they believed these were their only two avenues to success.

The summer that I turned seventeen, back in the early 1950's, our restaurant was facing a crisis.

On a Tuesday afternoon in early June, the truth was brought home to me: the Canton was running in the red. There was little hope that it would ever be restored to its past glory, when it fed the trainees from a nearby Army base, during World War II.

I had just graduated from high school, hoping that I might go to the university in the fall and meet some Chinese boys my own age. As it was, my life was waiting on tables, taking cash, and working the soda fountain. It was a warm day, and I knew this was the fateful summer. Would the lease be renewed by our landlord, Stanley I. Sorensen, the richest man in town?

Our restaurant—three floors plus basement—was owned by Mr. Stanley Sorensen, who came from one of the town's oldest

Norwegian families. He paid the water bills and the taxes, people said he was as rich as Croesus.

That day, *Ai-hao* (or "Big Mouth," as we called her), began the morning routine of filling the sugar bowls. She had worked in the restaurant since before I was born and felt she owned a share in its fate. Her real name was Iris and she was married to Peter, a barber. As usual, she was bossing me around, shouting about my negligence of the booths, the floors, and our well-paying customers.

"Hey, Ellenah, what's your station today?"

"The first five." (That meant the first five booths.)

"Your dad wants me to remind you to fill the sugar bowls," she said. "Mr. Sorensen is back from Norway, and you never know when he might drop in. If he doesn't renew your dad's lease this year, your dad won't have no money to send back to China."

She told me to clean off the counter so that the nice people in town would eat at the Canton instead of the Spanish dining room at the Hotel Albert.

I began filling the bus cart, nicknamed the Baby.

"And now the girls are talking about a union," Big Mouth added. "I don't think Sammy will have to worry about a union, though. He pays the highest wages in town. Forty a week plus tips. You can't do better than that nowhere."

She continued her monologue. "I wish he'd let your ma work in the back, though. He don't think it looks good. Well, the way I see it, she could dish up the *chow mein*. And it would sure make her happy."

I made no comment but helped her stack the cups and plates and saucers. She worked efficiently with a deft hand.

"I expect your ma's not as lonesome as she was when she first come over from China," Big Mouth continued. "You weren't born yet, but when I first saw your ma, she had long hair in braids. Now I hear she might go over to Al's and get herself a permanent."

From the kitchen came the smell of bacon grease. We took Baby inside and found Positive-Plus Uncle playing the numbers in the *China Tribune*. (He got his name from the Minnesota Health

Department, because he had a history of V.D.) "Yah, yah," he screamed, jumping up and down. *"Eynagamagahai."*

"Gambling again, heh?" Big Mouth said as she scraped the dirty dishes into the washer and helped herself to a piece of tomato. "That slot machine Sammy put in don't help your Uncle's bad habits none," she insisted. "I saw Reverend Olafson going over to the coffee shop to eat last Sunday. If your dad don't watch out, we're going to lose all our good customers. And that's no good when you want to renew your lease on this building."

The lease ran for five years, but until that summer I never realized why the lease was so important. But now Big Mouth reminded me every day. "Were you ever Chinese and wanted to rent a big store in a small town?" she would ask. (As if she knew what being Chinese was like!) "Hand to mouth begging," she'd say.

I sighed. I knew Mr. Sorensen owned everything. And this was the one place in town he was willing to rent to Papa out of the goodness of his heart. Everything else was rented. The American Federation of Labor leased the other desirable spot, and they'd held that lease for twenty years. "Only do you think those socialists would give that place up?" asked Big Mouth. "Don't you bet your Yankee Doodle Dandy." So this building on Main Street was the only place for the Canton. If we lost the lease, we would have to leave town. And where could we go? To Austin, twenty miles away? A friend of my mother—we called her Auntie Tong—and her husband owned a restaurant there. She had the packing plant trade sewed up faster than you could say "Hormel's Spam." Rochester and Fairbault and Mankato and Sioux Falls, South Dakota, were "sewn up" by the Chinese family of Tongs.

Of course, we could buy a building. But that took money, and money was one commodity Papa didn't have in his bank account. So, if we lost our lease, we lost our business.

I was quiet. I took Big Mouth's gossip for granted, just as I took the penny scale and the big snake plant Papa planted in a jug for granted. It was no secret that I handed Positive-Plus Uncle five bucks a month to play the Chinese numbers. Big Karl, chief of police, gambled with him too. You either played ball with Uncle or got lousy pork tenderloin sandwiches. You could kid Uncle about the numbers, but you got the best pork tenderloin sandwiches in town.

Our other waitress, a part- Native American girl named Helen walked by with a tray. Big Mouth was nasty. "You don't get the help you usta," she said. "Take that one. I betcha anything that she steals beer on the side."

Helen gave us a swish of her hips as if in reply. She was a very pretty girl with olive skin and high cheekbones, and she was getting prettier every day. Some customers thought she was my sister. "You have a very pretty sister," they'd say.

"She's a "w"_____" I muttered.

"What did you say?" Ai-hao asked.

"Nothing."

No doubt about it. I was jealous of Helen's beauty and how all the customers liked her better than they liked me. Besides the lease, there would be a new matter to worry about this summer.

Our town was old as Minnesota towns go—1865—the numbers read on the old county courthouse cannonballs. In the spring, the lilacs came in May, and in the winter, the snowbanks reached six feet—hot in the summer, arid cold in the winter, although spring was nice. Once in a while there was a tornado, and people remembered the years when tornadoes had struck and the names and background of the people who'd been killed. They also liked to recall the horrors of the town: Old Lady Lund, who killed four of her six kids with strychnine in their milk because there wasn't enough food in the house to feed all of them. The man they found dead in the bell tower of the courthouse. His face had been decomposed beyond recognition, so the coroner took a census and found nobody of importance missing. He figured it was a stranger.

In the white brightness of the June morning, I made my way

across Broadway and Main streets. Before me stretched a familiar
scene: the dusky shade of poplar and elm and cottonwood trees;
the public library with its facade of a lion's head carved near the
front door; the towering water carrier in the distance, symbol of
Franklin Delano Roosevelt and "creeping socialism." Ours was a
farmers' town and labor town that always voted the Republican
ticket in the state and national elections. In the spring the town
bloomed with lilac, and the perfume from the bushes spread like
creeping ivy as far as Main Street and the stores that led like
Hannibal's elephants up the hill to the lake region.

A block away, a girl I had known since childhood, Margie Jens
crossed the street. Now nearly eighteen, Margie was a plump, handsome girl with soft brown eyes and fat legs.

Idly I watched her make her way over to the dime store.

I remembered our growing up together, Margie's mother teach-
ing Mama how to bake an American cake and Margie's own inane
interest in learning Chinese words. I had neglected to get in touch
with her since I graduated from high school, but I told myself this
was because I was terribly busy. Actually the secret thought nagged
at me that we really had very little in common anymore.

Margie had changed little in all the years I had known her.
She was nosy and pert. From childhood her hair had been dishwa-
ter blonde, and there were still a few freckles on her nose. And she
didn't understand the expression "no can do." You might shut the
door, pull down the shades, and pretend not to be home, but
Margie would walk in anyway.

Margie was called "one of the Twelves" by Mama because she
was one of twelve children from a family that lived down the block.
When we were children, Margie used to come over every morning,
knock on a windowpane, and yell in imitation Chinese, "Gghai-
thleng-hoo chang jeep. Hey, Mrs. Wing, gimme some orange juice."
Most of the time, Mama didn't mind her, but once in a while she
got angry and chased Margie away with a broom handle.

I was about to cross the street when Margie saw me and yelled out, "Hey Wing-go-ching, where are you goin?" Brash and easy, she jabbed me in the ribs. "Don't take no wooden nickels."

"Oh, Margie, do you have to be so uncouth?"

"I don't know whatcha talkin about." She changed the subject. "How come you don't teach me Chinese words no more?"

"Because you always ask how to ask for food, that's why."

"Well, you should be glad I can talk to your ma," Margie said, grinning from ear to ear. *"Gghai-thleng-hoo chang jeep.* I ain't seen you at the beach lately," she added, as an explanation of her presence. "And every time I come to the Canton, you're not working."

"I've been busy," I said. "You know the lease on the restaurant is up," I added.

"Old Skinflint restaurant landlord" Margie said knowingly, "I hate him."

"I'm not worried," I lied. "He likes us."

"That don't mean nothin'," Margie said. "They liked my Pa at the packing plant. But they still laid him off."

She tarried, being a busybody.

"I haven't seen you at the movies lately either."

"I've been working."

"Is it true you're gonna go to college?"

"I've already told you, I don't know," I said wearily. "So what's new in your life, Margie?"

"I'm engaged," she announced. "To Ted Jones from Glenville."

"Really?" I was jealous. "Congratulations."

"We're gonna get married at City Hall, otherwise I would invite you. Nothin' fancy. My father kicked me outa the house." Margie's father was always kicking his kids out of the house. This was nothing original.

"Why this time?" I asked.

She leaned over and whispered into my ear: "Chingaling, we haveta get married."

I couldn't believe it. "You mean you got caught?" I said, whispering the new significance. "Where did you go?"

"Sometimes to Jugglin's. Sometimes out by the viaduct. Once

in the car. Once in old Petry's haystack. Come to think of it, it ain't all that great. But they say it is, and it's supposed to get better when you get more practice." She shrugged her shoulders.

"What's it like?"

"It's easy." She went into a detailed explanation.

I was shocked. "Oh," I said primly. "I think that's awful. How can you stand for it?"

After Margie left, I sneaked up Front Street, which was the back way to get to the town's public library. I passed the Milwaukee Railroad up near the Grainary, by the old people's hotel that Heinie Jenkins had put up for the Christian Science Church. I entered the familiar brick building named after Andrew Carnegie. The library was empty except for some tramps who liked to hang around the periodical room to study the maps of the world.

The librarian nodded to me in recognition. "Hello, Ching," she said. "I hope the family is well."

I nodded and headed straight for the stacks that carried my favorite book: *Ideal Marriage*. I took it off the shelf and hid it in a brown paper bag and went into the periodical room. Carefully I removed *Life* and *Look* from the rack and hid the book discreetly between these magazines.

I turned to the pages giving the different positions of the sex act and relaxed, greedily studying the pictures. Margie said she knew everything, or was she lying? Obviously it was fun.

"I hope your father and uncle know what you are reading," a voice said from behind.

It was the old-maid librarian.

"Papa says it's okay," I lied. "I'm going to college this year in September."

She knew my secret: I was a sex fiend.

If you think I was worried about losing the restaurant because Papa wouldn't have any money to send back to China, you are dead wrong. I was worried about the restaurant because it might put me into the poorhouse. That's what I think about in the wee hours of the morning—me.

One would think that being Chinese, I would be sweet and quiet. That is the front I put on because that is what is expected. I learned that a long time ago. "This is Ellenah," the teachers would say; "she is our Chinese student." And I would nod in gratitude for being allowed to be in the class. But underneath this sweet exterior, I am vicious. From the time I was tall enough to watch the cash register, I'd thought only of me—and boys—American boys.

When I was six, I had a crush on Jackie Davis.

In high school I loved Jim Jenner, who was a basketball star, and Adam Dupin, who was Jewish. Later, I had a crush on Nestor Gonzalez, a Mexican, on Robert Easter, a black. You might say that I did not distinguish because of race, color, creed, or national origin. But did they return my love? Never.

I was okay for doing their homework for them and singing in the chorus of HMS *Pinafore* under Mr. Ommon's baton. But I was no good for necking in Jugglin's Pond near Chicken Hill.

If you want to know whom I blamed, I blamed the Chinese. When I was little, I had read *The Five Chinese Brothers* and *Little Pear.* They had pigtails and all wore black shoes and went around saying, "Ah so," *and* "Ah lo." They were stupid. Since they were the only Chinese I read about in white books, I believed all Chinese were like that.

I used to march in the Memorial Day parade in my Chinese dress to please the Veterans of Foreign Wars and the American Legion. I was in the Girl Scouts and Campfire Girls and attended a couple of Christmas sermons at the Lutheran church. There I learned that Chinese weren't Christians.

So it was easy to blame the Chinese in China. I blamed both Communists and Nationalists.

I got to daydreaming. If it were not for the Chinese, I would say to myself, I wouldn't have to work in the restaurant.

If it were not for the Chinese, I could go bowling. If it were not for the Chinese, I could go to Schwen's Ice Cream Store and make a pass at Jim Jenner or Robert Easter.

They were fears, I suppose. Fears because I could not date white boys. (They might take advantage of me.) Fears because I could not date black boys. (They might take advantage of me.)

It was fear and jealousy that made me hate Helen, the beautiful waitress. She looked Chinese, only she was an Indian, Big Chief Wahoo. She never read any books and hardly spoke English, but everyone loved her—from Stormy Steene, the cab driver, to Ray, the silverware salesman. She was free.

Helen kept a room above a grocery store. I imagined her there in that room, raping men. Rape. Rape. To calm my nerves I would go to the basement and write graffiti in the ladies room. I wrote a lot of graffiti.

As I mentioned before, our restaurant was called the Canton in honor of the home town of Dr. Sun Yat-sen. "Canton Café" was advertised by the big neon sign that swayed in the wind. The restaurant was next door to Miller's Drugstore.

In the big window out front, Papa had installed a snake plant, a clock that he had bought in Minneapolis, a Coca-Cola sign, and three of the calendars he got free from the local milk company at Christmas time. I thought the window was pretty cluttered, but Papa said you had to advertise so that the American people would come in and sit around and have a cup of coffee.

During the twenty years he'd been running the restaurant, Papa had practiced what he called "good business," to draw in the American customers. Good business meant that if a man's bill was over a buck, I handed him a free cigar, and if a lady's bill was over fifty cents, I gave her a package of gum.

I don't know how well the system worked, but we got rid of a lot of gum and cigars.

Papa was even nice to bums. A bum would come into the restaurant, and Papa would greet him with a big smile and "Won't you sit at the counter, sir?" Then Papa would serve him a cup of coffee, a bowl of soup, and two-day-old doughnuts on a plate. Along with the meal, Papa would talk seriously to the bum about politics.

"Hello, young fellow," Papa always began. "You know that fight Chiang Kai-shek had with General Stillwell?"

Even if the bum didn't know about this fight, Papa would continue, "Stillwell in that fight all wrong. He not do very good job in Burma. He not do very good job in China. I feel he don't let Chiang Kai-shek fight the Communists."

"But when Japan fight in Indo-China, who surrender? When Japan fight in Burma, who surrender? When Japan fight in Indonesia, who surrender? But when Japan fight in China, did Chiang Kai-shek surrender? Did he? Did he, young fellow?"

That was the trouble. By the time Papa had pointed to the photograph of the Generalissimo that hung on the wall, the bum was scared out of his wits. No bum, as far as I can remember, ever came back for a second cup of coffee.

Papa was a short man with thick hair. At work he always wore a white busboy jacket, and he had the habit of bowing humbly when customers ordered *chop suey* and *chow mein* over the telephone. This bothered me.

It was this humbleness that made me believe my father lacked a certain basic common sense. For all his efforts he never could give his family more than pocket money. When Papa decided to help out Wimpy, the ragpicker, by buying bedsprings from him, they turned out to be too large to go through our front door. (We finally had to leave the springs in the front yard.) I thought of Uncle Lin Sen in Chicago.

He sold Papa three washing machines because he (Uncle Lin Sen) needed the money to bribe the immigration officials. We got the washing machines, but Uncle Lin got deported anyway. What bothered me most was Papa's biggest charity drive. Every Christmas without fail, Papa mailed three hundred dollars to Taiwan to help Chiang Kai-shek rebuild his army. I figured if you were going to spend three hundred dollars, why not fix up the living room? Or buy Mama some new clothes?

Not that Papa spent a penny on himself. He had only two suits and one coat to his name. Two suits in twenty years. That wouldn't have been so bad, but in spite of his thrift, the restaurant barely broke even.

CHAPTER TWO

Uncle Fung, Papa's partner in the restaurant, took charge of handling the meal books for the regular customers. He was a full head taller than Papa and vain. A favorite Fung pastime was standing in front of his framed B. S. degree in Business Administration from the University of Illinois. He didn't gamble; he never played the Chinese numbers, he didn't look at white women. He never smoked, he never drank rice wine, and he sent every penny of his savings back to his wife in Hong Kong to buy land. He wore horn rimmed glasses and spoke perfect English.

The people Fung most admired were the Epstein family who owned the Minnetonka Clothing Store and Bulbranson's Hardware. The Epsteins were good businessmen and ate three meals a day at the Canton. They paid cash on the barrel. They had also founded the Toastmasters Club. That meant a hundred dollars extra each month for the use of our balcony, converted by Fung into a "Chinese pavilion dining hall."

If you wanted to characterize Fung and Papa, you would say that Papa was all dreams and nonsense, and Fung was smart. Fung was a Wing, like Papa.

Though he and Papa belonged to the same family, Fung was not a true uncle in the American sense. Fung was also a martyr. He loved to tell anyone within hearing distance about his sacrifices for his wife in Hong Kong.

"How often I look at my wife's picture and wish she were here with me," Fung would reminisce. "She and my son, Thleck-see." That was the signal for him to reach in his pocket and pull out her picture.

"I have not seen her in years," he would say wistfully, passing the picture around. (I had seen it at least fifty times.) "She was a mere fifteen when we married—a true love match." Another sigh. "I must bear my cross, as Reverend Olafson says, until I can afford to rejoin them in Hong Kong."

Uncle Fung, being a college graduate, was the boss of the restaurant. Papa respected American college degrees. In spite of this they carried on a running battle over what Fung called "the restaurant bums," who frequented the Canton.

These bums charged their meals and used the restaurant as a free meeting hall for card games, idle gossip, and any vice that came to mind. You see, Papa couldn't say no to Americans. Fung couldn't say no to what he called "respectable Americans."

Fung said those bums made a difference between our family "making it" and "not making it" in the United States. Mr. Sorensen hated the bums in the restaurant. They were not respectable, and respect was important for *mien*. *Mien w*as one's honor, or "face." To my way of thinking, Fung made a lot of sense.

This difference, I discovered, was going to haunt me.

Papa's old-fashioned clock next to the pinball machine read two o'clock, Central Daylight Time, when bum No. 1 appeared. That was Olley Smith.

For the last fifteen years, Olley who played the organ at the Bijou, had always been at the restaurant at two o'clock, When he wasn't there, he was at the Hotel Majestic, where he lived as a permanent guest. He wasn't very good at paying up his bills at the Majestic, and once a month Papa would go over and talk to the manager about letting Olley stay on.

I tolerated Olley because of the talks we used to have about movie stars. Olley knew all about their sex lives, and of course had seen all their pictures. He was a dapper little man of Irish heritage, and the only giveaway to his poverty were the secondhand books he used to push off on Papa.

According to Henry, the hotel clerk at the Majestic, Olley's only possessions were a few foreign stamps, a bunch of autographed pictures from Ethel Smith, the organist, and a citation about his piano playing from somebody nobody had ever heard of. Henry swore that if you looked through Olley's hotel window, you could see him up at all hours of the night going over his newspaper clippings, talking to himself, and acting crazy in general. His books, his only luxury, were in a carton under his bed. They had been collected through memberships in various bookclubs to which he had belonged at various times. Olley, an avid reader, didn't believe in borrowing books from the public library. He believed in "ownership" of the "great masters." When he needed money, he'd sell the books to Papa.

Olley's need for attention was centered around the "local news" section of the *Tribune*. I had no interest in the daily goings-on of the town's elite families, but about this group, Olley had a relentless curiosity.

Daily, he would come to the restaurant, borrow some menu paper, and record with pen and ink the latest trip of some big shot to the Twin Cities or the potluck supper of some Catholic group. We never discussed the nature of the items, but it was my job to get him Papa's typewriter and wait until he had typed up each item. Papa would stick a three-cent stamp on the envelope and mail it to the local newspaper in care of the publisher—none other than rich restaurant landlord Stanley I. Sorensen.

"Hi, Ellenah. I have something for the *Tribune*," Olley said in greeting. "Three items of society. I know all about the history of this town."

Olley should have known better than that. The *Tribune* never printed anything Olley sent in.

"What are you eating?" I asked. I hated Olley. He never tipped and was very fussy about his food.

"Tea with toast and put a tin warmer over the toast, please, Ellenah."

When I came back with his toast, he was writing away. I decided to bring up an old beef.

"How come you just let me in to see the last half of the picture show?" I said. "If you had the kind of pull you say you have, you'd get me in to see the whole picture free."

"Ellenah, sometimes you remind me of your Uncle Fung, no gratitude. Now take your father, Sammy. There's a real gentleman for you." (Papa's name was San, but Americans always called him Sam or Sammy.)

He took out a book from his briefcase. "Tell your dad that I have the *Life of Andrew Jackson* for him."

"Olley, Pa hasn't read the last five books you sold him," I said. "You know his English isn't that good."

"Tell him anyway."

He looked up at the clock. "Oh, golly," he said. "It's almost four. I have to get back to work. I have a whole new set of songs on the organ."

"What about paying your bill?" I called after him.

"Just put it on the spindle, Ellenah."

I counted up Olley's bills. Almost a hundred dollars. Moocher! I thought. No wonder we were poor. Papa was a man without measure. "Be good to anybody who comes into the restaurant"—that was his song.

A voice from behind interrupted my reverie: "Ellenah, has the evening paper come in?"

The voice belonged to Doc Sorensen, our landlord's very poor cousin. His office was upstairs in the restaurant building, and every afternoon, rain or shine, he came in at five o'clock to read our local *Tribune*.

I handed him the *Tribune*. "Don't let Fung catch you reading it," I admonished him. "You'd better take it to the back booth near the kitchen."

"When's the family coming in?" He meant his own family, but this was a charade. Mr. Sorensen hadn't spoken to Doc in years.

"You know Mr. Sorensen comes in once a year at the end of the summer to tell us about the lease. That won't be for another two months."

He obviously wanted to talk more. "Going to watch the Fourth of July parade from my window?" he said. I hated his window— the ledge was filled with models of molars and bicuspids. "Sure thing, Doc," I lied.

Doc was a dentist without patients. Whenever he had one he would treat him or her to a glass of orange juice in the restaurant.

Scraps of past dealings with him marred my day. Can't you go away? I thought. Can't you see I have my own problems? Can't you give me some time to think about me?

That night, as they were counting up the cash receipts, Fung tried to get Papa to get rid of the charge spindle. He let out a yelp.

"Ew nega maga hei?"

"Look at that spindle! Bills owed by that organ player!" He punched his chest. "Remember Arthur Blowe? You let him charge, and he was caught forging checks in Saint Paul."

"Criminals!—we're harboring criminals at the Canton. No wonder we don't make a profit."

"The organ player's daughter does not recognize filial piety," said Papa.

Fung made a noise like Tarzan of the apes. "No other restaurant in this town practices charity. Take Pil, the Greek. He doesn't let the *huk-kai,* the blacks, eat at his place. But you, when Easter comes in, that *huk-kai,* you bow and call him Mr. Easter. Whoever heard of anyone calling a *huk-kai* janitor mister?"

Fung scratched his chest and wiped his brow. "Doc Sorensen's cousin is our landlord. His own cousin won't talk to him, but you let him read our newspapers. He takes the newspaper away from schoolteacher customers. Is that good public relations? Is that getting money for our old age?"

"Fung, what do you want me to do?" Papa said. "I cannot let Olley and Old Doc starve."

"Houston," Uncle Fung warned. "Houston, it will be this year if the lease is not renewed by Mr. Sorensen."

Houston, Texas, I thought wearily. Fung had some "rich cousin" there. From the way Fung told the story, this cousin was willing to give him a share in a grocery store. This cousin was always writing letters in Chinese to Fung, and the gist of the letters was always the same: "Dearest Fung. Come to Houston. We can cheat the *loothlong* (the Mexicans). We can cheat the *huk-kai* (blacks). We will just add a few dimes onto their grocery bill. They can't add. And the white stores won't sell to them. You will become rich."

That Houston trick always put the shiver into Papa. It was Fung's trump card, like the final shove of a victim over the precipice.

Like all minorities in town, we lived on the wrong side of the tracks. Our house was on Washington Street, between the Rock Island and Milwaukee Railroad lines. Our block was inhabited by one family of Indians, one family of Mexicans, and one family of Chinese (us).

The house was what you'd call White Minnesota Cape Cod, with two floors and a basement that flooded every spring. Papa had decorated it with second-hand furniture, including some Salvation Army castoffs, bought from Tom, a transient who rode the rails. But most of the pieces, including an old upright piano, Papa had gotten from the previous owner of the house, "the baby man." (Mama called him that because of his kewpie doll face.)

Mama hated the house. She hated the cold Minnesota winters and the sudden storms and the garter snakes you found in the basement in the summer. China was warm, she told us, not cold like Minnesota.

To appease herself, she saved everything. Life in China was hard, she said. Bandits came down from the hills in Toy San, her native village, and stole your money. "Put your money where you sleep," she cautioned. This habit persisted when she came to America, so that I imagined that her bedroom was filled with cash. Once I made a search. But all I found were boxes of free calendars donated to Papa from the Co-op Milk Company.

Mama always looked out of the window when she worked in

the kitchen. What she looked at I never knew, because an elm tree shaded the view of Mr. Olson's backyard. Always she seemed anxious—trifling over the size of a rice cake, re-tasting the Chinese frankfurters she hung above the sink to dry.

I often wondered about her life—not speaking English, getting matched up to Papa at the age of twenty, never having seen her husband until her wedding day.

It was her own fault she hated it here. She had refused to learn English. When I was a child, two Baptist ladies used to come once a week to plead for Mama's attendance in the church on River Street.

She went once—learned how to sing "In Christ There is no East or West," and then threw the hymnbook in the garbage pail. The ringing of the bells upset her sleep in the morning. ("Only the stupid Americans would ring bells for no purpose than to get people to come and sit for one hour and sing songs.") Another missionary lady visited her one afternoon and gave her a weekly reader and a sack of doughnuts. But Mama was in a suspicious mood that day and chased the missionary lady away with her broom. Mama insisted that she was too old to start anything new and, besides, knowing English hadn't made Papa a millionaire.

Actually she had little incentive to learn. She always assumed that when times were better, Papa would move to Hong Kong, where she could eat the sweetest oranges in the world and be rid forever of the American food that made her throw up. But Papa said that a woman belonged with her husband, and if she went to Hong Kong, she would get spoiled and play cards all day long and eat watermelon seeds. Lonely and rebellious, she began busying herself by growing Chinese vegetables and bitter melon in her garden and stealing tulip bulbs from Mr. Olson's shed when he was away birdwatching on Jugglin's Pond.

In the afternoon, rain or shine, she would take her "special" walk through the town. Down past the Rock Island Railroad tracks she would go, looking for some houses for sale. I couldn't get excited by any of them—they were usually shabby weatherbeaten boxes, made of "rare brick," an asbestos made popular after the Depression. But Mama always got carried away with their "revenue-earning possibilities." She figured if she could squeeze a thousand dollars out of Papa, she would put it down on a house and collect rent each month—at least forty bucks.

When the *Tribune* came out, she would make me read the real-estate ads to her in Chinese. While I read out loud, Mama would sit at the kitchen table, hungrily devouring the price of each piece of slumland she wanted to get her mitts on. "Repeat the price, Ching," Mama would insist in a loud tone of voice.

"Seven thousand, Mama. But it's been advertised before."

She was pensive "An old house. But I could rent it to the dishwasher. Or some of the Mexicans—when they come to onion weed."

"They just come up for the summer, Mama."

"What's the use?" Mama said, suddenly giving up the charade. "Even if it is for sale and even if it is a good investment, your crazy Papa will say it's no good or that he won't have time to look at it. If he listened to me once, we would be rich."

Mama was a witch. That was why she refused to go to an American church.

She kept an ancestral table. The porcelain kitchen god smiled down at us from a shelf in the kitchen. God of fertility and of family, he grinned the same stupid smile year after year, filled as he was with josh sticks and adorned with mama's hanging dried duck and barbecued pork. She also ordered ginseng root from Chicago and boiled it until the roots seemed to melt in the water. I was forced to drink the water when my head and tongue were parched with fever. She even hung grapefruit peel around my neck to keep away the evil spirits.

The one instrument in the kitchen I feared, however, was what I called the butcher knife—actually a Chinese cleaver. It was squat and square and sat on an *eemp,* a chopping block that had been cut from a tree stump.

Sometimes I held the knife in my hand—why I do not know.

Perhaps I believed that some of Mama's witchcraft would rub off on me. Perhaps for me, the knife was magic.

In all the years we'd been in Minnesota, Papa had conceded only one point to Mama. He allowed her to pick celery for the *chop suey* and wash dishes for four hours every evening. For this work, she earned fifty dollars a week.

The money she put into a safe-deposit box, for which she and Papa held a key. Every week she would gravely hand me the money, and together we would take it to the First National Bank on Main Street. I tried to get her to learn how to write her name in English so she could deposit the money herself, but she said it wasn't smart that way. The money was to help her get what she wanted out of life.

It was no secret, that wish. The money was to bring her nephew Ren-ren to America. Ren-ren was the only son of her only brother, who had been killed by bandits in China.

If Papa talked about Chiang Kai-shek, Mama talked about Ren-ren. "Let me tell you a story about Ren-ren," she would say. Usually I pretended interest. I did this because, when she told these stories, she made delicious rice cakes for me to eat. It made her happy to talk about bringing Ren-ren to America, so I tolerated it. Anyway, it would take Ren-ren years to come to Minnesota. The reason was because of American law.

American law (I learned from Papa) said that the Chinese were not fit to become Americans. According to him, way back in 1882, white people passed a law forbidding Chinese immigration. In 1924, these whites extended this law to include *nghetpun ngen* (the Japanese). But the way Papa told it, Chinese people were smarter than the Japanese. We found a way of getting around the law. This is what we did. Thanks to the San Francisco earthquake back in the early 1900's, we invented the *chee*.

The *chee* worked like this. A Chinese in the United States would go to the local authorities, say that he had been born in San Francisco, but that his birth certificate had been destroyed by the quake. Couldn't he get another one?

(For enough money, you could always bribe an American bureaucrat.) With this certificate, he'd apply for an American passport. Then he would visit his native village in China. Upon his return to America, they would report the birth of a son. This birth would be recorded in the U.S., for by law, the son was a citizen. In this way, a slot was created, which could be sold to anybody with the money to buy, and the resulting citizenship paper was called a *chee*. The buying and selling of *chees* became a way of life for the Chinese in America.

Mama was obsessed with the *chee*.

"Do you know, Ching," she would say, "your father is trying to get a *chee* for Ren-ren. Ren-ren has to study morning, noon, and night to learn the facts in this *chee*. He must learn the streets in the village where the ancestral tablets are kept. The immigration officials are very cruel, and we must be prepared to offer a very large bribe."

The recitation of these facts in the *chee* was called *seem ho-gung*. Mama repeated that phrase as often as she repeated the names of her family in China. That has nothing to do with me, I thought. Why does she force her alien world on me?

Since I was born in Minnesota, I hated to talk about slots. I felt it put us in a bad light, and one day, Big Karl, the chief of police, would arrest me as an accessory to the crime.

She said she was an Ong and would always be an Ong. Even if I had had a brother, he would have been a Wing, since he would carry Papa's name. The bloodline of Ong was her bloodline and must be preserved. This is where Ren-ren came into the picture. He was the only male Ong left in her immediate family. She owed it to her dead brother and to her dead father, to her family and to her culture, to bring him to America.

I thought she was crazy. At night, in my bed, I thought about it. She's Chinese, but I'm not, I believed. I'm American. I would like to be one hundred percent all-American.

My own feelings about Ren-ren were a mixture of curiosity and resentment. A portrait of him peered at me from the top of Mama's dresser, framed in gold and black. His fragile frame was slender; his nose aquiline. The suit he wore for the picture was too big (mailed by Mama from J. C. Penney's), and the pants covered his shoes. He looked awkward. To tell the truth, I didn't care if he never came—afraid as I was, that he had the upper place in my Mama's heart.

CHAPTER THREE

Even in the bright sunlight, the house had a deserted air. It had never been painted in all the years we'd been living there. "The junk house," I called it because of its second-hand furrnishings, which I hated. It was set almost below the water table and was hit hard every spring by the winter thaw. I remember sitting on the basement steps watching the water inch up to the top, wondering if we would ever need to rush for help from the American Red Cross.

As I walked up the path to the front door I noticed that the blinds were drawn. This meant that Mama had company—Chinese company.

"Why didn't you come on Monday? You usually always come on Monday," Mama was saying timidly to Auntie Tong, a thin, handsome woman with glossy braided black hair and gold earrings and gold bracelets. They were seated in the living-dining room. The house was cluttered—it was always cluttered—with false crepe flowers, the old upright piano, three tables, and all the restaurant chairs Mama could sneak through the back door without being caught by Uncle Fung.

An amiable smile and a cluck greeted Mama's question. "Don't you like it if I visit you in the middle of the week? After all, there are not many Chinese people around, cousin." (Like "auntie" and "uncle," "cousin" was a title of respect among Chinese.)

"Oh, Chingaling," Mama said when I walked in. 'There you are. Please get us some tea. Hot. And aren't you going to say hello to your Auntie Tong?"

Mama was always nervous when Auntie Tong visited us. The

lady had three beautiful daughters, whom she was grooming for the stage. One daughter played the piano, another the accordion, and one tapped and twirled a baton. So far, they had been paraded from county fair to county fair, but the only regular bookings were at the bandstand in Duluth and one honorable mention on the Major Bowes Amateur Hour.

Once a month I visited Auntie Tong and her husband Uncle Ting and their children in Austin. They lived in a stucco house by the railroad track. Uncle Ting had given his children rhyming names in English. "Easy to spell," was his explanation. So their white, prissy children were called Lory, Dory, and Mory. Auntie Tong liked to compare my attributes to Dory, who was a year older than I. Dory always came out ahead. Who could beat a baton twirler?

"It's inevitable," Auntie Tong said when I returned with the tray of tea and cookies. "You must learn English so you can take the citizenship tests. My dear cousin, all you have to remember is Secretary Steak. Like the piece of meat. Simple?"

"I have other things to think about. My husband and the restaurant," Mama said childishly.

"Don't pay too much attention to what Fung says Auntie Tong warned. "You know how he molds your husband. Demand that San let you work at the restaurant. I own one house of my own and have an electric sewing machine."

"Oh, it is not like China." Mama sighed heavily. "I tell you, cousin, this place is like a jail to me. Really, it is."

If Mama was requesting sympathy, Auntie Tong was refusing it. Instead she eyed one of the dumplings on the tray.

"Now, you don't put enough sweetmeats inside," she said, sampling one. "I make mine with a little more sweetmeat."

She returned to her topic at hand. "Ah, your husband, San, cousin," she said seriously, placing her neat manicured fingernail on another dumpling, "he lives in the past. He is always thinking about China, about Confucius, about the old values. You really should learn the ABC's," she continued. "It is your fault, partly, you know."

"Oh, my husband is not to blame," Mama cried out defensively. "It is just that he listens too much to that *tai huc san*—that college graduate Fung."

"Yes, I know," Auntie Tong said sweetly. She tried another dumpling. "You really should put more sweetmeats into this, cousin."

"Why did you not come on Monday?" Mama said again—as if that were her sole concern.

Auntie Tong gave Mama a weak smile. "I can take two days off now."

Slyly she opened her compact and powdered her nose. She said carefully that in business these days one had to experiment, make the menu more American. One had to—well, experiment. She closed her compact and regarded herself with satisfaction.

"Profits are very good for us," she explained. "We get all the packing-plant trade. And I never have any trouble getting cooks from the big cities. We even have Mah-Jongg in the back—very discreetly, of course."

Outside the windows I heard a car sweep past on the road. Auntie Tong rose then and looked through the curtains to be certain that her car was safe, gleaming in its chrome and fresh paint.

"I have more problems than you do," Mama said, stirring her own tea with a glass spoon. "After all, I have been waiting so long for my nephew to come from China. He is the last living male in my family line." She spoke about her favorite subject without too much complaint.

Auntie Tong nodded with seemingly patient understanding.

"In America," Mama continued with a painful twinge of remembrance, "we wait for our relatives. We are in a jail here, but we wait."

"What news do you have of your nephew's coming?" Auntie Tong said after a sufficient pause for Mama to collect her fine grievances. "What is his name again?"

"Ren-ren. Ong Ren-ren," Mama said with great feeling. She said it the way some Christians say "God in heaven." "But he will be coming soon—soon," she said flatly, now that the question had been asked. Somehow the whole situation was shameful, admitting that Papa had been too slow in getting the necessary groundwork done. It was not to be explained, exposing our family ailments. "Naturally I hope it is this year—this year," she said, her voice trembling a little.

"I see . . . mmm," Auntie Tong said, sipping her tea with birdlike movements. "It is a shame that your brother left only one living son."

Auntie Tong paused. As always, she was right—she had assembled her life with efficiency, and the next words were predictable: Mama should know better. Mama was too soft with Papa. A woman should manage a man, like mastering the English language or learning how to type the ABC's. Auntie Tong could preach because she laughed at the old ways, she lived each day without sentimentality, without emotion. She had told Mama this in many meetings before, and she would say it again. Was security not life? she repeated. Was this not the only way?

"I hear your restaurant lease is up for renewal," Auntie Tong said now. "Ahem, dear cousin, I hope there will be no problem with the American owner of the building?"

"Of course there will be no problem," Mama said proudly. "Mr. Sorensen, the landlord, likes my husband very much."

"Of course, dear cousin," Auntie Tong said cheerfully.

Finished with that topic, Auntie Tong shifted to another. "I suppose you haven't done anything about finding a good husband for your daughter?" she said carefully, almost too casually. "I must say, how old is Ching now? She must be at least nineteen by the Chinese calendar."

It was a dig.

"My husband may decide to send her to college," Mama said. "These are modern times."

"But if there is no new lease, there is no college," Auntie Tong said a bit maliciously. "You know, even the people in our village in

Toy San are talking about this. Your husband's false pride, it stands in the way of many things—many good things."

"I don't care what they think back in China anymore," Mama said then. "I've been here in the Gold Country so long that one forgets."

"Of course, my dear," Auntie Tong replied carefully." . But then you were always more of a mouse than I. You never learned the English language, and you never use people who can help you. And you never use the proper force, the proper tone with your husband."

Auntie Tong shifted a well-stockinged knee. She examined the large diamond on her hand.

"In America, wealth is measured in diamonds, not in jade," she said. "But in other matters, the cultures are the same. To have your own house, to have a sewing machine, to have your daughters marry well, to have your family around you in your old age.

"Now you take my husband. He does whatever I tell him to do. The old ways do not work in a new country, and one must always be practical about matters. Look. You have wanted your nephew, the last of your family, with you for how many years? And your husband is still fixing up the papers. Now your daughter is of marriageable age. She does not have much of a dowry because of your husband's values. You must do the thinking for both of you."

"I'm doing all right," Mama said again.

Auntie Tong's pretty mouth turned up at the corners. She stirred her tea and said nothing. Her eyelids closed. She was quite pleased, it seemed, with the private realization that she had more of everything that was important than Mama.

I decided to make my escape. I was nervous when Auntie Tong talked about finding me a husband. Her daughters all were engaged to men of substance, but none of them had gone to college. Even though Papa talked of my going to college, of my being treated like a boy, I secretly envied Auntie Tong's daughters, the swiftness in which life was laid out for them. Why did I have to have my particular father? He was head of our family *tong,* our association, but what good was that if you had no power in other matters?

I marched up the stairs to my bedroom, a tiny attic nook

It was the smallest room in the house, furnished with Papa's castoffs from the restaurant and what may have been given to him by the Girls' Friendly Society. I kept my room neat except for one corner, in which I heaped movie magazines. I spent hours late at night going through the magazines, daydreaming about Hollywood and swimming pools and visits to a motion-picture studio. For safe keeping I kept the diary I wrote in a closet. It was the usual romantic girl stuff, filled with exclamation marks, dreams of conquests by male movie stars, and hopes of the knight in shining armor. I examined my figure carefully, pulling in my stomach and tracing the cups of my breasts. I jumped when I heard a knock on the door and I scrambled into a bathrobe. When the door opened, I looked up and saw Auntie Tong smiling at me.

"What are you doing, Ching?" she asked.

"Nothing," I said. What was I to reply—that I was admiring my brains and wishing my body would get skinny? That I hated her pretty daughters who tapped and played the accordion? (I especially hated the daughter who jumped up and down with her baton in front of the Memorial Day Parade.)

"I'm studying Chinese," I lied. "I have learned how to write the characters for filial piety."

"I haven't had much chance to talk to you since you graduated from high school," Auntie Tong said kindly. "You were number one in your class, your father said."

"Number two," I corrected.

"Any nice young man on the horizon yet?" she asked. It was her favorite subject, tabulations of men that she thought were worthy husbands for me.

"I told your mother that I would be happy to be the go-between if you would like to meet Mr. Lok-fat of Chicago," she continued. "Now that would be a good husband for you." She looked in her purse for a cigarette lighter.

"He certainly is rich enough. I believe you may have heard me mention him. Mr. Lok-fat owns a soy-sauce factory in Chicago. And he has property. He even rents the basement of his apartment house to Mexicans—although they don't make good tenants. I told him he should rent only to Chinese.".

I said (bravely I thought), "I don't want anybody to pick a husband for me. I am a modern girl." Then I added defiantly, "In America you marry whom you please. You pick each other."

"Perhaps," she said. "But this is easy for beautiful girls. Let us face it, Chingaling. Your face is too round. You are a little on the fat side. And forget about those Northern Chinese men you might meet at the university. They are all snobs."

"I'm certain there must be somebody who would like me," I said then. "I've read a lot of books."

It was a stupid remark. Again I attributed it to Papa's upbringing. He was always telling me to go to the library to study, always saying that it was better to study at the library than go bowling with the American kids. Books? But did study ever bring a girl a husband?

"Yes, Ching, you are intelligent," Auntie Tong agreed. Then she laughed merrily. "Aren't we all, though, dear?" she said easily.

She then gave me a firm motherly talk about men in general. There was no need to be hoity-toity about it, just because I was going to college. Naturally, I should go out only with the highest type of person, not one of the cooks or one of those crazy Communist students from China—but somebody nice, somebody professional, from this country. Her daughter, for example, had done very well for herself—even though Auntie Tong had picked the husband. There was no harm in a little modest matchmaking for anybody

"American born" or not. And Mr. Lok-fat, whom she knew personally, was a man of the highest order. (She had sold him a very large insurance policy.)

"I don't say you shouldn't meet the person and make up your own mind. But let me tell you, your parents know what is best. At least your mother does. You could consider it, Chingaling," Auntie Tong continued, looking at me carefully. "After all, it is not easy to find a good husband these days.

"I am not interested," I said matter-of-factly.

"Ah, my dear, my dear," Auntie Tong said in the voice she would use to coax a child. "That is what my oldest daughter said before I introduced her to Lee Shee." She gave me a secretive look. "His father is a wealthy manufacturer in Hawaii." She reached into her pocketbook handed me her future son-in-law's business card. "They have a nice house in Phoenix," she indicated, showing me a photograph in gray, brown, green, and red of a brick ranch house with her daughter in front of a Lincoln Continental. What more could a girl ask for?"

Then, confidentially, allowing the message to have just proper effect, "But once she had ideas like you. 'I am a modern woman,' she'd say. "I want to make my own way in life. Besides, you want to please your Mama, don't you?"

"My father wants to send me to college," I said.

"Nobody's forcing you into anything, Chingaling. Nobody at all." She took out a compact and powdered her nose carefully.

"What is there really in this world," Auntie Tong reminisced, "but security? Money? Being an individual is hard, and most young girls don't know what they want. Someday," she said, while she applied fresh lipstick, "you will know what I mean." She paused. Inspiration had ceased. She pulled the photograph of her daughter from her purse again, looked at it with approval, and returned it to safekeeping.

In my dresser mirror, she regarded her own profile with approval also. She was very handsome and she knew it.

"My dear child," she said then, "you drink too much cow's milk. It's bad for your skin," She looked at her watch. "It's getting late. I have to go up to Minneapolis and help them pick celery. My husband has a large share in the Shanghai cafe there, you know."

Several days after Auntie Tong's visit, I came home from the Canton and found we were not alone in the house. A fat stranger was sitting on our living-room sofa, chewing watermelon seeds. He was methodical in his attack on the seeds. He would chew one and split it open. Then he would chew it again. I found him very ugly.

I went into the kitchen. "Who's the uncle?" I asked Mama.

"That is Mr. Lok-fat of Chicago." (Aha! I thought. Auntie Tong!) "He is a widower. He served in the United States Army in the Signal Corps. He owns a soy-sauce factory in Chicago. And he has a building in New York City on Mott Street."

She was very excited and pale, like a young girl. "I'm going to change my dress," she said, "so go in and be respectful. I want you to make a good impression."

Suspiciously I returned to the living room. "Good afternoon, Uncle," I said.

"Ha," he smiled. "A fat girl. I like fat girls."

When Mama came down, she wore her best pink dress from J.C. Penney, Inc., and powder and lipstick. The powder was sprinkled lavishly on her cheeks. She looked like a piece of peppermint candy.

Lok-fat nodded to me. "Hi, fat girl," he said. "Your mother has written me a letter about you."

"Ching, get a tray," Mama said anxiously. "Tea is good with sweetmeats." She began to talk quickly: "I have heard ridiculous rumors that you may wait until Chiang Kai-shek wins back the mainland before you remarry."

Lok-fat shrugged his shoulders.

"On the other hand, I understand your caution. Many American-born girls are wild. They do not listen to their elders. They like to spend money on clothes. They like to ride in airplanes." She nodded in my direction. "My daughter is not like that. She speaks very good Chinese. She reads and writes Chinese. She is not like those *chuk-sing*, those bamboo heads."

Lok-fat seemed to agree. "She is a nice fat girl," he said, pinching my cheeks. "I hear you read and write good English. You can help me with my business."

"Number two in her graduating class," Mama boasted, offering him another cup of tea and an orange.

"On the other hand," she went on, "you do not want a girl from Hong Kong, either. They are from the big city. They spend money. My daughter has learned thrift. She knows how to take cash. She has been taking cash in the restaurant since she was ten years old."

Instead Lok-fat studied my legs. "Nice fat legs, too," he said. "I like fat legs."

I was miserable. He reminded me of all the restaurant cooks who used to come to visit from Chicago and New York. And he was fat and old. Mama was no help. She was giving me orders to show him around the town, since there was no work for me in the restaurant at this hour.

Then I knew. I was to be matched in marriage to this awful person. If I did not do something desperate, I'd have to sleep with him. I had to do something. But what? I was powerless.

"Before you leave, Ching, play the piano," Mama said. "Show Mr. Lok-fat how good you are at playing the piano."

I went alongside Lok-fat for the first block away from the house. Underfoot the sidewalk was cracked. I tried the Chinese style, two paces behind him. But he wanted to be democratic.

'We go together, fat girl," he muttered jovially. "I can take you to the motion-picture show.

Ahead of us was the long slow trek up the hill to Main Street. I tried to point out the landmarks: the water tower by Franklin Delano Roosevelt; the Elks Hall; the pool hall where you paid two bits for a mug of beer. But Lok-fat had eyes only for me. 'He pressed my hand and kissed my knuckles. I felt like a piglet being prepared for slaughter. I began to squirm and feel awful.

Olley, the organ player, was standing in front of the theater wearing a straw hat. "Hi, Ching," he greeted me. He tipped his hat to Lok-fat. "Hello, hello."

Save me, save me, Olley, I silently cried. Pretend that seats are filled. But Lok-fat pressed a five-dollar bill in Olley's hand quicker than you could say Jack Robinson. What did he care if half the picture was finished? Gallantly, Olley escorted us into the darkened arena.

We were seated near the aisle. I pressed myself into my chair. But the hiss of "fat girl, sweet girl" could be heard from his lips. His hand pressed my hand, grasped it, held it, squeezed it like a limp orange. I wanted to scream, but no noise came. I have to get away, I thought. I have to talk to someone. I leaped up from my seat. He didn't catch up with me until we were out of the theater in the fresh air.. I knew then that I had to confront Mama.

I got the courage to speak to her the following day. I was measuring her height. She enjoyed this ritual; if pressed hard enough, she might stretch to five feet three. She was proud of her height and spoke of it often. She was an inch taller than I, which proved her point that cow's milk did not add inches to one's body. Cow's milk merely made you throw up.

"You're still taller than I am, Mama."

"I knew it," she said triumphantly. "That cow's milk doesn't do you any good."

"I didn't enjoy the movie with Lok-fat," I said suddenly..

"Girls only think they have to know someone first. Since when did knowing someone make you happy for life?" was her reply.

"Many Chinese girls these days pick their own husbands."

"And how many of them are happy? How many of them are secure with rice to eat?"

"What if I never get married?" I said.

"That won't happen if you let me pick your husband."

"What happens if I don't marry the one you pick?"

"Don't come to my doorstep and ask for a free bowl of ice," she answered prophetically. "If your Papa has his way you will probably be an old maid. He says you should go to college. Since when did college find a good husband for a girl?" She shrugged her shoulders. "But if you want to make life hard for yourself, that is your decision. Although I should hope you will not be as stupid as your father, not as impractical." I left her and went into my bedroom and sat down. I fixed my hair. I cursed the dreariness of my life—the airless room, the bare windows and the ironing board. I stood naked for a full minute before the floor-length mirror.

I jumped when I heard a knock at the door.

"Ching," Mama hollered through the door. "Your papa says Ren-ren will come to America. If he comes, I don't care if you marry well. You can go to college. With Ren-ren here, I will have done my duty to my dead father and dead brother."

There it was—Ren-ren again. He was a part of my life—someone I did not know, someone whose picture was in every room of our house, whose name was always on my mother's lips. In the front of my mind, a thought churned: Ren-ren, you in Hong Kong, I wish you were dead.

CHAPTER FOUR

June ended. We began smuggling firecrackers into the restaurant. The month that had started with some hope came swiftly to an end.

I could tell by Uncle Fung's irritation that he was beginning to worry more and more about the lease. "I think we'd better call Mayor Johnny," he said to Papa. "Get Ching to get him on the telephone."

Mayor Johnny had never actually been elected to office, but he was a perennial candidate and friend to the Chinese people—or so he kept telling us. He was Papa's lawyer. To tell you the truth, when you needed him, Johnny Thorhold was hard to find. Since he wasn't in his office, I figured he was at the infamous Palm Garden with one of his lady companions. The Palm Garden was infamous, so Big Mouth said, because it catered to the unwholesome elements in town.

At first we couldn't find Mayor Johnny.. "Are you sure it isn't the real mayor you want?" a strange man inquired. Then a woman's voice came on the line and said Mayor Johnny hadn't been seen in that vicinity since last March.

At long last when Papa was beginning to worry, Johnny's familiar baritone came booming over the wire.

Papa anxiously told him about our great worry over renewal of the lease by Mr. Sorensen. Johnny replied that he had been called to City Hall to advise the administration on new taxes, but out of pure love for his Celestial friends, he would come to the Canton immediately.

Whenever Johnny came to the Canton, he always sneaked up

to a waitress and tried to talk her into accepting a box of nylon stockings from him. You never saw a man go after a girl with nylon stockings the way Johnny did. When he couldn't get a date with the stocking trick, he would give the box away to the Girls' Friendly Society.

Johnny had a round face, a round stomach, and he always carried a round cigar. He was pretty tall, but he liked to wear vests, even in hot weather, and a homburg hat, which he always tossed into the air so that it landed squarely on a peg by the snake plant.

Johnny was a nuisance, however, when it came to his flirtations. You see, he liked the beautiful waitress, Helen.

"Hey, Ching," Johnny said when he arrived. "That waitress has a nice back.

I frowned. "She wears it like a signpost."

Johnny didn't say anything He just smacked his lips "I'd say she brings in the packing-house crowd. Good stock. Yankee and Conquistador as well, I would imagine. She is a very pretty girl. Chingaling, do you think she would accept a box of nylon stockings from a gentleman and a scholar?"

"In the back," I said instead. "Papa and Uncle Fung are waiting for you."

"No need to fear, Johnny is here," he said, flipping his hat in the air and watching it land squarely on the peg.

"Bring me back a plate of beef stew with a little pat of butter on the side, please."

As was his custom, he then walked over to a shelf under the cookie counter and pulled out a whiskey bottle. "Safe and sound," Johnny said, wiping the bottle with a handkerchief. "Every year, the good Lutheran ladies keep this town dry, but someday, when I am mayor, it will all be changed." He kissed the label lightly. "Can't keep the old ticker going without some pepper-upper."

When I frowned, he just smiled. "Remember—a little pat of butter on the side, please."

When I brought him the food, Johnny had all kinds of charts and graphs spread out in front of him. He was telling Papa and

Fung not to worry. "All's well that ends well, to quote Shakespeare, that great bard."

Anyone might suppose it was possible Mr. Sorensen might not renew our lease, but the chance was remote. Who else would want to rent this building? No one. The town was a dairy center and there already was one dairy. Nobody wanted more industry. Life was settled and secure. And wasn't Mr. Sorensen from an old family, and weren't there arguments for that?

"Class, Sam," Johnny said seriously, "always shows." He took a spoonful of stew. "I feel there is nothing too much to worry about. The restaurant, it is true, is not doing as well as it did when it fed our great American army, but then we must make some sacrifices for peace."

Johnny thumbed Papa's ledger carefully. "From the books of your ledger, the sale of meal tickets is going well." His thumb scanned names and addresses. He took out a pad and scribbled. "For example, Miss Macdonald, the little lady pilot—a toothsome lovely. And this name is nice too." Hastily he jotted more addresses down on slips of paper, which he slipped into his vest pocket. "Aha, where were we? Oh yes, the lease." Now Johnny handed some figures to Papa.

"Sam, you gross at least six hundred dollars on Saturday night. Add that to Sunday's four hundred, and show that to Mr. Sorensen. Those are the figures he likes to see. And you've always been prompt with the rent, always prompt."

"You the boss, Johnny," Papa said with reverence. 'You tell us."

"The lease has lapsed before," Johnny continued, quoting from his last Toastmasters Club speech. "And Mr. Sorensen is a gentleman and a scholar."

Johnny penned the word "COURAGE" on the ledger. "I feel that under the stresses and strains of modern life, everyone tends to worry too much, feeding himself the horrors of the possible, without considering the probable." he paused. "Do you understand the point?"

Papa said he did.

"In life, there is always this element of chance," Johnny continued soberly. "But I wouldn't worry about it yet. Your old lease"—pause—"I have the precise facts at my fingertips, still has some time to run." Johnny looked at the calendar. "It's June. Plenty of time."

Johnny motioned to me. "Ching, tell that waitress Helen to bring some ice back here, please."

Now he looked down at the ledger. "Mr. Sorensen is a friend. He is a man of heart and good business sense. All we have to do, Sam, is continue to give him Chinese gifts from your homeland . . . porcelains and vases."

"As long as you say so," Papa said to Johnny. "You our advisor."

"STANLEY I. SORENSEN." Johnny penned his name next to "COURAGE." How many years had he leased the building? Nearly twenty. That was a great record. How often had the lease been renewed? Like clockwork, every five years. Chew that for two minutes.

Johnny then asked Fung to name all the Chinese gifts he had bestowed upon the restaurant landlord since we had come to live in the town: three embroidered dragon panels; ten gallons of oolong tea; two kegs of *lichee* nuts; three carved inlaid ivory-and-teak tables; five dozen ivory figurines; four porcelain lamps; three Chinese screens. "Friends," Johnny concluded, "that's an impressive list."

Johnny then pointed out how we should prepare for Mr. Sorensen's visit. The local packing plant must send the best aged steaks. Uncle Fung should buy yellow crepe paper streamers and a red-and-gold Chinese sign with the lengthy greeting: "WELCOME, RESTAURANT LAND LORD, HONORABLE STANLEY SORENSEN."

I, with a volume of *Familiar Quotations,* should compose Papa's thank-you speech for the renewal of the lease. It as important that everyone memorize his part.

"Let me do the talking with Mr. Sorensen," Fung advised Papa prudently. "My advice is that we should say nothing about the lease per se. I will talk about other matters. No doubt Mr. Sorensen will bring it up himself."

Johnny nodded in agreement. "And find some excuse to give them the presents, Ching—the box of lichee nuts and the oolong tea. It's the gesture that is important to the Sorensens. The gesture—and above all, be humble."

The lease disposed of, they went on to other items on the agenda—the bills to be paid, the restaurant supplies to be ordered. Actually, Johnny spent all his time ogling Helen.

"That waitress does have a nice back," Johnny repeated.

Papa frowned. "I hire her on your recommendation, Johnny," he said.

Johnny helped himself to an ice cube.

"But she bring in customers," Papa admitted.

"I would say she's very good for the packing-house crowd, Sam," Johnny said. He smacked his lips again. "Nice pedigree, very nice." He leaned over and put his hand on the chair.

"Hey, Ching, remind me to buy some pure-silk stockings for that girl; not nylon, silk. I'd like to measure her foot, heh, heh."

"Size nine and a half," I said haughtily. "And you have to stand in line, Mayor Johnny."

"You mean she has other admirers?" Johnny laughed jovially.

At Papa's look of guarded censure, I shut up.

Papa avoided quarrels with Mama by being in perpetual motion. It was a built-in shelter from her anger, as much a part of him as brushing his teeth in the morning at the kitchen sink. He awakened promptly at nine o'clock, rushed into the bathroom, got into his clothes, and plucked his Chinese newspaper, the *San Min Chin Pao,* out from the vase, all in about eight minutes.

Witnessing this familiar scene, Mama maintained a stony silence until Papa was well out of the house.

"Look at him go," she would then shout. "His legs can't carry him fast enough to the restaurant. He has put all his faith in the Americans and in their goodness of heart. Since when did goodness of heart put rice in one's stomach?"

According to Mama there was no time for fighting except at night. Papa came home at about three in the morning, after mopping the floor and counting up the money in the cash register, and then she would get after him.

The adjoining room where I slept had paper-thin walls. That night I could tell by her greeting that he had been summoned to the battlefield.

"Papa, how were the profits today?"

"Oh, okay." (He never told her. The profits were always okay.)

There was a long pause. I knew Papa was tuning her out by reciting Dr. Sun Yat-sen's Three Principles to himself, his head propped up on a wooden pillow.

"Papa, if profits were good, you can fix up the paper for Renren. We have almost enough in the cash box. If you can't, I have a plan for him to go to Canada. I will go up to Canada and sneak him over the border if you will just give me the car fare."

"You talk like a crazy woman," Papa answered. "All these years I have been busy making a living and being head of the family of Wing. You still curse me for that?"

"And what is your record of bringing over relatives? Just Positive-Plus Uncle, who can't even get a clean bill of wealth from the Minnesota medical board."

Papa murmured something I didn't catch.

"Auntie Tong said that Ren-ren can sneak through the Canadian border if you cannot buy a slot for him," Mama continued breathlessly. "Americans say all the Chinese look alike, and we can pass him through the inspection like he was a piece of meat." She was very excited. "Last week three people did it, Auntie Tong told me. Papa, what do you think of that?"

"I think you're crazy," Papa said. "You can't go to Canada. You can't even speak English."

"That's what you think. I'm not a coward like you. And just

because I can't speak English doesn't mean I'm dumb." It was conversation I had heard before.

"I remember how when Ching was a little girl you said she had to go to school," she continued, "or the police would get after you. Do you know that Mrs. Gin from Mason City never sent her daughter to school? And Mrs. Gin found a very rich husband for her daughter from Hawaii. Do you know that the boy came over from Hawaii to meet the girl in an airplane?"

"Oh, woman," Papa muttered.

"You are afraid of the American police. But do you think those border police frighten me? If I get in trouble, they will put you in jail. Not me, but you." She continued in this strange excited tone. "And what do you think about that loss of face?"

"They matched me up with a crazy woman," Papa repeated. "In Toy San they matched me up with a crazy woman."

"I must look after my daughter, if you can't," Mama said. "You have always been so impractical."

There was another silence. When the conversation resumed, however, Papa was doing the talking for a change.

"Normally, I do not interfere with the ladies who come to visit," he said, "but I want to tell you that I disapprove for their acting as a *moy-ren* for my daughter. If you must consult the charts and the stars and matchmakers, wait until she is of age."

"Of age?" Mama demanded. "In the Chinese calendar she is almost nineteen years old. I will die without having any cookies to eat from giving a daughter in marriage.

"Auntie Tong is willing to act as a go-between with Lok-fat," she said. "Lok-fat is a very rich man. He owns a soy-sauce factory in Chicago. I have heard he has a Japanese and a Filipino partner."

"Auntie Tong exaggerates," Papa said.

"She may exaggerate, but she has done well by her daughters. You said her baton-twirling daughters were not better than *moo-loo-chahs*. Well, they may be dancing girls but they have found good husbands to give them new lives. They have found fiancées with money and position."

There was silence. But what I heard next warmed my heart. "Lok-fat is too old for our daughter," Papa said. "He is not a good match, and I forbid it. I have other plans for her."

So Papa had spared me from a matched marriage. I must thank him. But in my heart of hearts I wanted more. I wanted a knight in shining armor.

As long as I could remember, from the time I was tall enough to reach the cash register, my conversations with my father had been limited to politics. They were odd discussions, since Papa did all the talking and I just listened and said yes and no at different intervals. But before he started on politics, I had to do what he called *niem shee,* or my recitation of his Chinese lesson for the day. Since we lived in Minnesota, where there was no Chinatown and therefore no Chinese-language school, he believed it necessary to teach me himself. He did not wish me to grow up to be a *chuk sing,* or hollow bamboo head, as the people from China called the American-born Chinese.

The conversations—if you can call them that—took place in the back booth at the café. Papa kept some inkwells here, and he regularly ordered Chinese books from Hong Kong for my benefit. "Ching, bring me a pot of tea," Papa would say. And then, "Recite the lesson for today."

He never spoke during the recitation. He nodded, sipping his tea, never interrupting, unless I did not know a word or faltered at a certain character. Mama approved of the Chinese lessons, but she felt Papa's lectures concerning politics were stupid.

It was customary for the Chinese part of the lessons to last no more than half an hour. If Papa was unusually tired, having worked very hard all day, he would sit quietly, close his eyes, and recite the lesson along with me.

Then abruptly he would stop and say, "Ching, close the book. That is enough recitation for one day. I want to discuss philoso-

phy with you. I want to discuss philosophy because I believe you
are old enough to understand the challenges of history."

"The challenges of history" is how he put it. But 'Chiang Kai-
shek talk" was how Mama and I put it.

But that part of the lesson could go into two hours if there was
a slack period in the restaurant.

"Now. I am not going to say that everything Chiang Kai-shek
ever did in his life was all good," he would always begin Part II.
"But a man has a right to make a few mistakes n his life; and who
alone fought the Communists for twenty years."

"Chiang Kai-shek, Papa."

"That's right. Just as in politics, the important thing to remember in life is that there are certain things that are right, and
certain things that are wrong. This is what good parents teach
their children."

And that was normally the end of the conversation.

Until the previous year the routine of these talks went un-
changed. Then abruptly Papa had discontinued the Chinese lessons. But the political sequences now were never more deliberate,
almost desperate—as if the noise would divert him from darker
thoughts. Lately, when he said, "Ching, bring me a pot of tea," I
sometimes sighed, hoping Fung might call him and divert his
attention to some restaurant matter. I did not enjoy our talks.

That night, he took the pot, let the green leaves settle, and
then proceeded to pour himself a cup. He sipped lowly. But he
did not talk about Chiang Kai-shek. Instead he thrust an American newspaper, the *Minneapolis Tribune,* under my nose. "Trans-
late into Chinese for me," he commanded.

The headline said, "Americans Help Chinese War Hero Fight
Tuberculosis at Goose Lake Sanatorium."

I read the article out loud to Papa. I explained that it was
about a Chinese Air Force pilot named Mr. Kiang, who was at the
sanatorium up at Pine City, and he had a wife and baby who were
boarded with a farmer nearby on Route 1.

"It is as I thought," Papa said when I had finished translating.

"It is the one I read about in the Chinese newspaper in San Francisco. He fought with Chiang Kai-shek. He is the one who wrote to me. I was just talking to your uncle about it last night. How strange that a hero with Chiang Kai-shek should come to Minnesota and that he wants my help. It was your uncle who suggested that you be relieved of your waitress and cashier duties and be allowed to journey by train to this town to write letter for him and his wife in English and to help him on questions of his health he may have for the American doctors."

I was speechless.

"The problem," Papa continued, "is that the Americans are hearing about their misfortunes and are sending them money—dollar bills through the mail. And the Madame does not want charity. She heard about my reputation as head of the family Wing. She heard about my honesty and my trust. Even though she speaks English; she cannot write English very well. She trusts me to send the money back for her."

His face glowed from considering the trust the Kiangs had put on his shoulders.

"Yet she wishes to thank the Americans for their kindness and their generosity," he said. "And since I am too busy to go, and the lease may be renewed any day now, I allow you to go in my place . . . to represent the family of Wing. It is a great responsibility."

"When do I leave?" I asked feebly.

"Day after tomorrow. I need you to work Sunday the split shift."

He seemed enthusiastic about my trip. "You won't need much money. And you have a chance to ride the Rocket, the fast train to Minneapolis, where you change. I'll have the kitchen fry some chickens for you to eat on the road."

He scratched his face, which still glowed. "And remember to carry a pillow. I always carry a pillow when I go to Chicago to count money for Uncle Lok at the laundry. The conductors on the fast train charge fifty cents a pillow."

I rose, thinking he was finished with the talk, but he touched my hand lightly, almost affectionately. This was a rare practice. According to Confucian custom, Chinese parents do not touch their children.

"Daughter," he said, "wait. I want to talk to you about the American Presidents." He put on a pair of reading spectacles. But he didn't read anything. He just lectured.

"Lincoln, Franklin, Jefferson. May Taft be next President. Their life very important. And what most important quality in their life?" He paused to pour some tea. "You think because they smart? No. Because they thrifty. They have money. Every one them. You, my daughter, might think different, because you go American school. Not true. I know Jefferson very thrifty man. You think I not smart because I don't go school. Where was I?" he asked.

"You were talking about the American Presidents, Papa."

"Your mama not read many books. She not know about the importance of education. Your Mama thinks I too slow about doing things. It because she not read many books. And I think it important for my daughter to read books, get education like she a boy. I have decided to send you to college."

I was stunned.

"You want to go, don't you? Education and scholarship made your Uncle Fung brilliant."

He must be crazy, I thought. Uncle Fung was just brilliant enough to save his money and say, "Two, this way please" to the American customers. You didn't have to go to college to learn that.

"China very poor," he continued. "If you study and make A's in school, someday you may go back to Free China. Yes, with your education you may help China, like Sun Yat-sen helped China. If Mr. Sorensen renew my lease, I think I can save enough money to give you to go to school. How you like go east, to Habold College?"

"Harvard College doesn't take girls, Papa."

"Well, you make up mind. I'm sure Mr. Sorensen come through. You think about it."

Papa rose. He took his teapot and cup into the kitchen That meant the conversation was finished.

Dutifully I took the trip to Pine City, wrote letters for the Chinese colonel and his wife, and sent the dollar bills back to the kind American people. Papa insisted upon paying the postage for these letters, and the colonel and his wife were grateful, saying *sheh-sheh* in their soft Mandarin dialect.

When I returned home, Mama was in very good spirits. Normally not a good housekeeper, she suddenly dusted the chairs, framed a lot of pictures of relatives to put up on the wall, and spent hours at the table writing letters in Chinese. The reason for these new undertakings was not apparent until one day, when I got home at about three in the afternoon to rest up a couple of hours before returning to the restaurant to work the night shift.

She was making rice balls in the kitchen. They were little larger than eggs and filled with pieces of chopped pork and *cha shew* (barbecued pork). She's happy, I thought. Something is up.

I found out soon enough. She had circled today's date on the Chinese calendar and written across it: "the white man."

"The white man" was Mayor Johnny. I had forgotten about the appointment. That meant she had enough money for the false citizenship paper for Ren-ren, saved up in her treasure chest at the bank.

"Hurry up, Ching," she called to me, putting some powder on her face. "Get me my pocketbook from the hook in the closet. We are going to see the *chung chloo* today. Then we will go to the bank to get the money in the cash box to pay for the false citizenship paper."

I brooded for a moment and reluctantly followed her out of the house. It would be good to have the money matter finished. Perhaps this would ease her obsession.

Mayor Johnny's office was on top of the AF of L building next to Phil's Café. The sparse furnishings and the "Yours truly Eugene V. Debs" autographed picture suggested hardship, but I knew that it was Johnny's flair for affectation. There was the bear that Johnny had shot in the North Woods, now a peaceful rug on his floor, and photographs of Johnny's parents and grandparents.

Johnny was most cordial when he ushered Mama into the office. He pulled out the chair for her, set her comfortably so her feet touched the bear rug, and brought her a glass of beer.

"Well, well, well, what a nice visit. I bet your mother doesn't remember the first time she visited, or, I should say, set foot in this office. That was a long time ago—a long time ago."

"What's he saying?" Mama asked anxiously. "What's the lawyer saying?"

"He's saying how happy he is to see you, Ma."

She smiled back. "Tell him thank you."

"Mayor Johnny, my mother's thanking you," I said.

"Mama, he wants to know if you remember when you first came here."

"Of course I do," Mama said. "Tell Johnny he wasn't so fat then. But even then he smoked cigars. And he gave me some towels and his wife made me some doughnuts. Tell him that I remember when his wife made dresses for you and gave you Shirley Temple dolls."

These preliminaries over, Johnny went to a file cabinet. The drawer was labeled "Chinese Clients."

"Ah, Ching, tell your mother it hasn't been easy," he reminisced, going through the file. "It's not like pulling a rabbit out of a hat. But you must admit I've helped a lot of Sammy and Fung's family in my time."

There was Uncle Jim in South Dakota—income tax evasion. Johnny remembered that case. There was Uncle Lee Wing in Iowa, whose son had been caught robbing a dry-goods store. Johnny had gotten his name off the police blotter. There was the case of bigamy of Uncle Been Dee in Minneapolis, who insisted upon bringing two of his wives over in the Brides Act. It had not been simple, helping him.

"You think that's simple?" Johnny argued. "Try to do it

yourself." Particularly since the Chinese were too proud to go on welfare. Johnny liked dealing with minority groups. I fact, it would be a pleasure if we could get some more Negroes and Mexicans in town, flood the place. Then Johnny would have the minority campaign sewed up for sure.

"Mama came to see about Ren-ren," I said, bringing him back to the subject at hand. "Did you fix up things with Papa?"

"Of course I have. Have I ever failed the Wing family", Johnny said. "But you have to admit, this was a particular tough nut."

Johnny told us the best time to talk to Papa and Fung about the intimate matter of Ren-ren was at night, when the restaurant business had died down. At half past ten, when he arrived, he would tell Papa that he had given the matter of Ren-ren his full attention. For two weeks now, Johnny said, he had been corresponding with Ren-ren's future "false father in California." He had composed a dossier of *what* Ren-ren should learn about his "parents"—their habits, their love for fast cars (they had two). Johnny had photographs of them in their home to send to Ren-ren which he could show to the immigration officials.

Johnny rummaged through the file cabinet some more. Things weren't very neat; he took out one folder after another and returned each one to the drawer. "The folder is here somewhere," he kept muttering. "It's got to be here." Finally he pulled out a brown manila envelope with the expression of someone extracting gold from a tooth.

"Ah, ha," Johnny said. "Just the family to sell a false birth certificate to your Mama. The family of Ong Be-lai. Same family as your Mama and Ren-ren, the same given name—well, almost the same given name. Cen-men is the name. An easy name for Ren-ren to remember and to adopt. Cen-nen—or Ren-ren to become Cen-men—was born eighteen years ago in Macao." He handed Mama the envelope.

"All we need to complete the transaction is a small check for only two thousand dollars. I will discuss that with him when I next see him and Fung. Tell your mother, it is on my calendar in black ink."

"Did you tell him to match the ages as close as possible?" Mama interjected. "I see you're not telling Johnny anything," she chided. "That's the trouble with you, Ching. You just don't like to interpret English for me."

"I tell you, Ma, Johnny has everything right there in his folder. If you could speak English, you would understand."

"Did you tell him how old Ren-ren is really?"

"Ma, he knows." I had lost patience.

Mama handed Johnny one of her photos of Ren-ren. "Now explain to the lawyer that the papers do not have to be exact. Just so there is no problem that Ren-ren will look the boy's age. The best paper is one that says twenty years old. That would be the best."

At that moment the telephone rang. I could tell by the way Johnny was talking that it was one of his Palm Garden Ladies. I knew then that the meeting was over.

"Tell your Mama that one of these days when I am mayor, things will be different," Johnny said. "Then we will have people in Congress getting through new immigration laws so that there will be a better quota system for the Chinese. Tell your Mama that."

"What's the lawyer saying?" Mama said all the way down the stairs. "What's Papa's lawyer saying?"

She left Johnny's office confident of her family's future. 'How many hours I have worked for this day," she said. 'Ren-ren will come to America. We have the money in the cash box to pay the false father and enough left over to bribe the immigration officials and the people who work in the consulate in Hong Kong." She bent over to smell some roses.

CHAPTER FIVE

The next day there was great excitement at the Canton. We had some Chinese visitors from Minneapolis and New York. The older man wore a long mandarin robe and got a lot of attention from Uncle Fung who bowed three times from the waist. And the younger man was the best-looking young man I had ever seen.

"Who are they?" I asked Big Mouth.

"That's the Honorable Ah Ling Tang, head of Hi Sing, and that's his son. He calls himself Bingo," she explained in a somewhat awed tone.

"Why are they here?"

"The Honorable is holding his association meeting here," she said. "And his son is going to spend the whole summer at the Canton." She smiled. "Maybe you will have a boyfriend at last."

Hi Sing? I marvelled at the name. Hi Sing was the terrible rich tong that allowed gambling. Papa had reared me on the evils of Hi Sing and the difference between our goody-goody family association—which was broke—and Hi Sing, which reached like an octopus into small businesses.

The difference, Mama always said, was because Papa was against gambling.

Wing Association lent money without interest. Wing Association needed only a man's word. Wing Association fed the poor. But Hi Sing? Hi Sing was a "corporation" that lent money at outrageous interest. It permitted gambling and paid off cops to exist. From the way Papa talked, Hi Sing was a den of drugs and prostitution, a place of "bad women" and "dancing girls."

I was curious to see all this vice. I was particularly curious about the dancing girls. I imagined half-veiled women sitting around with opium pipes, playing flutes and blowing smoke rings from long cigarette holders.

"That Bingo boy's been in trouble," Big Mouth said.

"What kind of trouble?" I asked.

"Girl trouble. What else? He went out with some white waitresses. I hear he got two of them in trouble. Anyhow, why else would a rich man's son like him spend a whole summer in this godforsaken town?"

"He doesn't look like he's so fast," I said. "I think he looks very distinguished."

"Well, if your dad is as rich as the Honorable, you can afford to be a ladies' man," she admitted.

While we cut butter, she told me what she knew about Hi Sing. The association Sing owned supermarkets and movie houses in Arizona. The Honorable had made some very profitable land investments years ago, when land was dirt cheap in Arizona. My father was head of an association, but it was small compared to Hi Sing. It was all very exciting.

Helen, the pretty waitress came by. "He's cute," she said. "I mean the son."

Helen would know. She'd go for a man at the drop of a hat.

I squirmed. "You'd better get them some set-ups," I said.

"Sure, Chingaling."

"I whispered. "Double w_____.

Bingo Tang. It was a nice name. I wrote the name twenty times on my waitress pad. Next week I would go on a diet.

Big Mouth was right. Why would someone like him come to our small town? Then I thought, Bingo might be a young hatchet man. He may have had to shoot somebody or avenge a crime and may be in hiding here. I imagined a Robin Hood running around a Sherwood Forest filled with evil crooks and pirates. That reason was good enough for me.

According to Mama, the Honorable was the number-one king of all the families of the Middle West and the West. At one time the Honorable's family fought tong wars in San Francisco, Chicago, and even Minneapolis, but there was now a truce among all the families.

With peace, the Honorable's tong had prospered, branching into the Southwest, owning lands and grocery stores in Arizona to cheat the Mexicans and grocery stores in Houston to cheat the blacks, the *huk-kai*. With envy and slight bitterness, Mama told me how Hi Sing got big pigs cooked at New Year's time and delivered many cakes to many weddings, while we, the Wings, remained poorly and low. Hi Sing had a ladies' guild, which had pictures of Madame Chiang Kai-shek in its meeting hall. The Lady Hi Sing, as it was called, had founded three Chinese-language schools, one rhythm band, and three dragon parades. It had donated funds to buy two fighter planes to help the Chinese Nationalists in their fight for freedom against Communist China. Although none of the ladies ever saw these planes, they played Mah-Jongg day and night and waited for news that Chiang Kai-shek had stormed the Chinese coast.

People only speculated about the money in the Honorable's coffers. Some put it at two million, others at ten. They told of its powers when some uncle, a poor cook at the Kunchu in St. Paul, had thwarted the family and was killed. Other gruesome stories were uncovered, but as Mama said, that was part of the past; now was the time for all families to get together. Weren't we all Chinese in one family in America? Shouldn't we all have a rice bowl of roses?

As a gesture to all families, the Honorable had picked our restaurant in which to celebrate his business pacts with Benny Wing of Sioux Falls, with Jack Wong of Rochester, with Ben Lem of Oskosh, Wisconsin, and John Gee of Minneapolis. The deals extended to mutual help and the buying of shares in soy-sauce factories, bean-cake mills, movie houses, real estate, and slum properties in Chicago. For days before the arrival of all these Chinese, the Canton was in a state of agitated activity. Under Fung's orders, we closed for three days—an unheard-of policy. I sat in the back booth, shelling nuts and making *won ton* patties.

The front windows of the restaurant were framed with Chinese Nationalist flags and other patriotic red, white, and blue bunting. In the dining room, there was a large portrait of Sun Yat-sen, the Generalissimo, and Madame Chiang.

I had never seen so many Chinese people. They came from Austin, Mason City, Minneapolis, and St. Paul, from Milwaukee and Duluth.

Uncle Fung greeted the men with a grin and a smile like a brightly washed blue-willow plate. Mama was Sherlock Holmes. She tracked down the home village of every woman who came, she remembered every temple, every store, and every road in a place called Chek Hom, where they had brought the pigs to market. She jostled babies and listened to the women talk about their "American" jobs in sewing factories and bobby-pin plants. I kept away for fear the women would ask me to teach them words in English.

Then the telephone rang. Mama answered the phone and then she got preoccupied.

"That was your father," she said to me. "He can't come because he has just had an attack of asthma. He wants me to bring him some food home in a paper carton."

I went to the soda fountain and began drawing water for the tables. I felt it was a shame that Papa would miss the biggest celebration in the life of the restaurant. But then it was like Papa to be unlucky with his breathing just now.

In the kitchen, Positive-Plus Uncle and the men cooked *da-bing loh,* the traditional fish dish that you dipped in boiling water with chopsticks and ate with lettuce, peanuts, and rice wine. In a corner of the kitchen, the women made *chow fon,* the soft noodles, rolling them out from the rice dough, eating mooncakes while children clustered about, eating Popsicles. Auntie Tong did not work, but supervised, philosophizing to the women around about my unmarried state. "Do you think your daughter will get a rich husband with her brains?" she said to Mama. "Get her a husband who will buy Ching a house which she can rent. Money, that's all that matters in this world."

Mama only smiled, obviously in good spirits. "I make an American cake yesterday," she said.

"How was it?" Auntie Tong asked.

"Oh, very good," Mama said. The Twelve family used to use only three eggs when Mrs. Jens showed me how to make a cake. I used six eggs in my recipe. It made the cake *ngeen*, so soft. It was more delicious than the cake baked by the Twelves."

"How do you manage to get the ingredients?" Auntie Tong asked.

Mama laughed. "Ching takes me to the stores—although she is difficult. She is afraid to speak up. If I could learn a few words of English, I could do my own shopping." She shrugged her shoulders. "It's a good thing. I am so strong. Any other wife would have hanged herself under the same conditions."

"Your husband is to blame," Auntie Tong said, recalling some of Papa's mistakes and failures of the past. "San is not a very practical or courageous man."

"Oh, San is not that stupid," Mama said in a fierce show of loyalty. "It is just that he listens too much to the Americans. He thinks they know everything."

At that moment there was a hush in the room. "He's here," one of the ladies whispered, "in his fancy car. How *sa-chien,* how important!"

It was sleek and black with curtains. "A Cadillac," I decided, "or maybe a Lincoln Continental."

The Honorable entered, followed by an entourage of men, all bobbing up and down like porters at the Albert Hotel. As usual, Uncle Fung led the parade.

"*Suk, suk,*" he kept mumbling over and over again, "uncle, uncle," as he shook the Honorable's hand. "An honor, an honor."

The Honorable reminded me of pictures of Chinese mandarins in his black high-button frogged suit and his soft Chinese slippers. It was known that he seldom wore Western dress at these banquets. His face was very aristocratic with its high cheekbones, thin lips—he was a contrast to Fung, who kept wiping his forehead with a handkerchief.

"A splendid gathering, well-planned, Fung," the Honorable said genially. "I am truly flattered. I wish all my enterprises were planned so well. But that is the hospitality of the Wings." He took a seat with Fung in the first booth, while Fung beckoned me to bring over a pot of tea.

The Honorable smiled when he saw me. "How is San's daughter?" he asked me. "I hear you did very well in your studies. It always pleases us elders to know that the American born are doing as well in their studies as their counterparts in Canton and Shanghai."

I blushed and said nothing.

"I hope you are getting along well with my son," he added, as Fung pulled out a chair for him. "Your Uncle Fung and I are going to talk while the food is being prepared. Why don't you pull up a chair and join us."

I felt uncomfortable but did his bidding. Bingo had already joined some boys in the kitchen.

Fung and the Honorable seemed to get along very well. They talked about the assets of mutual families. When the Honorable discussed his own family, he called it a "tax-exempt organization."

"So, how is San's family doing in business?" the Honorable said when I brought the family pot over to the table.

"We just about break even," Fung confided. "We don't have the soldiers anymore like we did during World War Two, and the Toastmasters are planning to move their meeting over to the Albert Hotel next year." He leaned over and added some sugar to his cup. "You know that our family is waiting to hear about the renewal of our lease from Mr. Sorensen, the restaurant landlord."

"Labor Day, isn't it?" The Honorable raised an eyebrow. "When the American gentleman comes for his free dinner."

"Usually he comes before, but this year I tell San not to count his chickens before they are hatched. Mr. Sorensen is getting on in years."

"Well," the Honorable said, "remind me to send you a note about that. I have some ideas on the matter that I could share with the Wing family."

I was ill at ease. The two men talked in riddles.

"Do you still tell San about your threats to go to Houston?" the Honorable chuckled.

"I tell him. That brings him around usually, but this year I am worried."

The Honorable addressed me, "Well, we have been neglecting our little girl who makes all A's. How are you?"

"Fine," I said, not really knowing what to say. "Just fine."

At that moment there was a stir in the dining room. Food was served, food in all the booths and at all the tables upstairs—pressed duck, bean cake, rice, all the flavors and condiments and goodies of Canton. After everyone was seated the Honorable nodded. That was the signal for the men to challenge each other to drink *diew* (whiskey). Who could drink the most at one gulp? Jimmy, a self-announced hero of the Burma campaign, began the betting. "Japanese battleship," he hollered in English as he raised his fist. "One, two, three . . . I challenge Ben Lee!" Everyone laughed as Ben Lee took the challenge.

After dinner, Bingo came over to his father's table. He was carrying a set of ledgers. I got up.

"Don't go," the Honorable said. "Our business is open to everyone to see." He winked at me. "Besides, don't you want to see what an intelligent son I have?"

"Some of the affiliates are wondering about allowing Americans into the fan-tan games," Bingo said. He sat down.

The Honorable shook his head. "No. Definitely not. By habit our players go to the same table. They are discreet. They are known to each other. It would be unwise in the long run—in spite of early profits."

"Some places are complaining about the cost of police protection," Bingo continued.

"I was afraid of that. Get off some community project to the police. The good policemen can save face. Perhaps we might picket the precincts near our gaming tables and demand more protection. What else is important?"

Bingo glanced around. "You might think this idea is foolish, Father."

The Honorable pressed his fingers together and took some tea. "Speak up," he said.

"Well, the term 'Benevolent Association' has come under suspicion by some snoopy American sociologists," Bingo explained. "It is being said in newspaper articles that benevolent associations are not benevolent and that they are tongs."

"I see." The Honorable seemed pleased that Bingo brought this up. "What would you suggest, son?"

"I thought you could change the name to the Hi Sing Veterans Association."

The Honorable seemed puzzled. "Most of our membership were not active in the war on the front lines. But I'm curious. Go ahead."

"The membership does qualify," Bingo corrected. "They were members of the Signal Corps." He grinned. "Cooks."

"Ahhh. Of course."

He repeated the branch of the service several times. "A nice patriotic gesture to the Americans. We could march in the Fourth of July parades and other parades. We could set up some games right in the American Legion hall. We could begin our own post— we will name it for a member who fought in the service and died in the war for the American cause."

"Oh, yes," Bingo said. "There must be a couple."

"Anything else, son?"

"We have our lawyers working in Washington to try to change the immigration laws. In the meantime, the Lins need their mother over. I was thinking of a church sponsorship. Could you talk to the American reverend?"

The Honorable pondered. "The old China lobby. Thank heaven for good American friends. I will try Reverend Snyder. He loves children. His church could sponsor Mrs. Lin under the Refugee Relief Act."

"In the meantime, the Lees are afraid. The immigration officials are bothering them. They live in fear of being deported because they have false papers."

"Tell them they have no fear. If they get harassed, we will handle these officials. We have not broken any laws. You know what to do."

"We also have ten new war brides under the War Brides Act. They need work."

"Okay, get them into the cookie factory or the bobby-pin factory. American wages are better. And tell that union official, no monkey business."

They talked some more, but the most interesting part was finished. Finally Bingo closed the ledger book, rose, nodded to me, and went to join the other men in the kitchen.

Business over, the group got loud and boisterous. Men and women wandered around, drinking whiskey, whispering secrets. Some of the cooks listened while Positive-Plus Uncle told jokes in Cantonese. Some of the cooks undid their shirt buttons, baring thin chests and no hair, in exaggerated gestures of comradeship. One small man kept popping pictures with his Brownie flash camera.

The Chicago group went to a cabinet and took out some equipment. I recognized the standard stuff for fan-tan—the large green felt tablecloth, the long stick to count out the beads, the little cups that looked like fingerbowls.

Bored with it all, I went to a corner and sat down at a table, hoping that Bingo would come and join me. Instead, there was a slight slap on my shoulder, and I looked up at the Honorable peering at me with a slight smile.

"May I sit down?" he said in English. "We really didn't get acquainted yet. I was so busy discussing business with your Uncle Fung."

"I want again to remark on how pleased I am that you did well in school. But I am not surprised, with the man who is your father being your teacher."

Was I hearing right? I thought. Papa being my teacher? Papa,

who discussed only politics and unrealistic nonsense like how won-
derful the Nationalistic party was in Taiwan?

"I know your father well," the Honorable continued quietly.
"It is a good table that he has set for my flock." He smiled again.
"We were boys together, although he came from a different village.
Your father comes from the village of Toy San in Pak Sa. But as a
boy I used to visit his village. Even then he was a man of very strict
principles."

Why was he talking to me about Papa? But since I did not
know, I nodded. "Yes, sir."

"I would like to tell you a story about your father. Everyone
knows this story, and that is why he was picked to be head of the
family of Wing. There was a ne'er-do-well in his village, a parasite
who did no work. Nobody would lend him money because they
knew the money would never be returned. But since he was a
member of your father's family, your father lent him money. The
man died, and left a widow and children. Your father gave the
children jobs in the restaurants owned by the Wings. But he for-
got about the loan."

"Just like Papa—stupid," I whispered in Chinese under my
breath.

"He is a Confucian in the strict sense," the Honorable continued, taking out a package of cigarettes and using a holder for one.
He puffed a few times. "You probably don't know this, but your
father is the only banker I know in America of Chinese descent. In
private, we call him the Bank of China. From all over the United
States, men send your father cash for safekeeping. They put it in
his name for their families. Why do they do this? Because he is the
only man they know who will not take their money and use it. He
knows that he is trusted by all of them. They know he will keep
their money and give it to whomever they want. And he demands
no money for his services. It is for him a question of honor."

My father, the Bank of China? And he without a cent in his
pocket? I refused to believe it. Yet I knew it was true.

"He is like a priest in the American society," he said. "When a man wishes to make up his will, he goes to your father. He tells him the will. It is oral. He gives your father his earnings and his money. It is all in trust to him. In all these years he has never faulted. Yet there has never been a written contract."

The Honorable rose. "Well, I have talked to you as if you were my daughter. And I have filled your head with talk. But again, you should be proud to be the daughter of your father."

I was shocked at the confidence given to me but more shocked at my reaction. Papa was a little stupid not to accept any money for his services. Whoever heard of a will that was given orally?

Mrs. Ding came over and asked me to fill out her Social Security forms. That done, I was about to get away when Bingo came over. "Scotch and soda," he said, handing me a drink. "You said you wanted to learn how to drink. I say, just a little at a time."

"I had a nice talk with your father," I said.

"That's great. He's quite a guy."

"He talked about my father. Isn't that funny?" For a moment Bingo's eyes were dark and brooding. "I think your father is really very nice," I said. "And everyone is nice to him."

"People are nice to him because they're afraid of him. It's because he runs the association."

"My father's head of an association too, but nobody is afraid of him."

"That's because your father doesn't believe in gambling," Bingo said. "You can't make any money in an association if you don't gamble."

He began to explain the associations to me. Normally I would have found this tedious, but I liked his handsome eyes and his beautiful face. I just looked at him while he talked.

Back in China (in the village), families lived together. Family associations were formed to help each other out. Immigrants brought this idea over to America. So if you were a Wong, you belonged to the Wong Association. If you were an Eng, you belonged to the Eng Association, and so on. If there hadn't been discrimination in America, the associations might have dissolved like sugar in water, but since there was discrimination, the Chinese got together even more. The associations protected you, gave you money, helped you find work. Some associations made money. Some associations didn't. It was all very logical.

"Does your father really have that much power?" I asked.

"Look at the way people jump when he snaps his fingers," Bingo said. "And you're just seeing the best side of him. He can be difficult when he wants to be."

"Where's your mother?" I asked.

"She's in Hong Kong. She's not the first wife. She's the *ngee*, the second wife. Now that's another difference between your dad and mine. Your dad brought your mother over."

"Personally, I think my mother would rather be in Hong Kong. She's always talking about it."

"Maybe she's not as unhappy as she says," Bingo said.

I decided to go back to what was really on my mind. "I don't think I could ever talk to my father like you talk to yours," I said. "I just wish once he wouldn't begin a sentence with 'wipe off table,' or 'bring glass water here to old Doc,' or 'nice day, ain't it, young fellow.'"

"Maybe someday you two will talk," Bingo said.

"How would you like a father who everyone says is crazy?" I said. "Imagine sending all your money to Chiang Kai-shek."

"How would you like a father everyone fears, a father the cops are always after?" Bingo said instead.

"Oh, that's nothing. The cops are after all the Chinese up in the Twin Cities," I said matter-of-factly, "because so many have false papers. Everyone knows that."

"What do you say when people say that your father stole money from the people? And that they are just waiting for him to slip up or get killed or for you to slip up or something? How would you like that?"

"He looks like he can take care of himself," I said. And I let the matter rest there.

At about eight o'clock, the Honorable left with several of the cooks. Uncle Fung and I saw him off in his big black car. After he had gone, the others returned to their drinking and card playing. Then I noticed a strange thing. Papa suddenly appeared in the restaurant. It seemed he had completely recovered from his illness.

The Honorable's visit had a peculiar effect upon Mama. She began wearing rouge and curling her hair. She would sit before a small cracked mirror in her bedroom and issue commands to me to bring out the curling iron. Patiently, I would wind her straight hair around the burning tongs until I got a small ringlet. When I was finished, she would wind a pink ribbon around her head and smile at her vision in the cracked glass.

One day after this operation she bade me get her pocketbook, which was on a top shelf in the closet. "We will visit the bank with the Indian head," she announced. (The Indian head was the emblem of the City National Bank of Minnesota.) "It is time I took out the cash for Ren-ren's paper to give to the white American lawyer."

Obviously her counting on the abacus had reached a lucky number; or perhaps her staring at the stars and reading charts and graphs in the Chinese newspapers had signaled some lucky day, some full moon or eclipse that had special significance. Anyway, I did her bidding. I saw her rouge her lips and wet her hair and sprinkle powder on her face. That meant we were "going uptown" to the bank.

The American bank frightened me a little with its look of authority. It had a marble exterior; the entrance had a brass plate that shone like the helmet of a Roman gladiator. I imagined big chunks of bullion and mounds of cash sitting in steel vaults.

Mama smiled as we approached the cashier's window.

"My mother wants the key to her safe-deposit box," I said solemnly to the clerk.

"Okay, Ching." He went over to another clerk sitting at a desk.

They whispered for a few minutes and then the first clerk came back. "Isn't that the safe-deposit box that Sammy and your mother have together?" he asked me.

"Yes."

The clerk looked at the man with the bigger desk. "Come with me," he said. "Sammy and your mother have Box No. Three-twelve."

We were escorted inside the inner sanctum past the first door and the big iron gate, which opened with the push of a buzzer. Wow, I thought to myself, all this money! At that moment the clerk pulled me aside.

"Chingaling, I think I'd better tell you before your ma finds out. Your dad came in the other day with Fung, and they took some of the money from the box to fix up the tables and chairs that they were buying for the private dining room they are fixing up in the balcony."

"Papa took some of the money?"

The clerk nodded. "I think there's only a few hundred left in the cash box."

Mama let out, a cry like an animal caught in a net. I didn't have to tell her. She was counting the money over and over.

"Ma," I said feebly, trying to explain. "The bank said that Papa needed it for fixing the restaurant."

"Fixing the restaurant," she echoed. "When he doesn't know if Mr. Sorensen will renew the lease? See what putting all that money into the restaurant will do for him? See what happens when you count on the white man? See what will happen?"

I calmed her down by getting her to go around the block. I cursed Papa for forcing this duty on me. The restaurant was his responsibility, but Mama was mine. Why didn't he take care of his wife? Why did he always put her on my shoulders? I was going to call the restaurant and tell him this to his face. I would say, Papa, she's your wife. I'm your daughter. But of course I didn't.

Mama was never one to sit quietly and read Chinese newspapers when she felt herself wronged. But she never challenged Papa in front of company and kept her fights with him behind their bedroom door. This time, however, she had no compunctions about bringing it all out into the open. She started in on Fung, whom she believed to be "cured meat"—easy prey. She was waiting for him when he appeared, as he always did at 3 P. M. to sample her sweet dumplings.

"Do you know that my husband invested all the money we saved for Ren-ren's *chee* in the restaurant?" she demanded.

He was quiet. That meant he felt guilty. He drank some tea and ate another dumpling.

There was a long silence. Mama held herself upright against the back of the chair. "I was talking about it to Papa only last night, and he didn't mention that he needed the money for the restaurant," she said. "He talked as if he was getting ready to give the money to Johnny, and Johnny was going to forward it to the false father."

"San did not want to hurt you," Fung said. "You know how soft-hearted he is. Look at it this way: Without the restaurant, you will never bring Ren-ren over. It is just a matter of time."

"He was lying to me."

Uncle Fung shrugged his shoulders. "You are too dramatic," he said. "It is a matter of logic. It is a matter of priority. Your nephew is still young. He is only twenty-two by the Chinese calendar—that makes him only twenty by the American calendar."

"What about Papa helping over that member of your family from Minneapolis? He got to America. And they only began working on his false papers a year ago. Or was it because you were the one who sold them the false paper? Very funny—that your wife should have had triplets and the immigration officials believed you."

"That is beside the point," Uncle Fung said, pressing his fingers together tight. "They needed a paper for a ten-year-old boy. My papers were for a son of that age. I cannot help it if your nephew was too old to qualify for these papers. Do you think that I discriminate? I would have been happy to sell you my papers."

Mama snorted. "So what about Mrs. Chin's nephew? He got to America. And they just found a slot for him over a year ago."

"That is beside the point," Fung repeated. "But then you never did see things logically. You are too emotional."

He began to pace the floor. "It was San's decision. He felt the money should be put into the restaurant overhead for emergencies. I admit that I feel the same way. But that does not mean that someday Ren-ren will not come to America."

He paced some more, then paused dramatically. "What if Mr. Sorensen says that we have to remodel the restaurant or we won't get another lease? This is our means of living. Where would the family be without the restaurant?" He wrote some Chinese characters down on a piece of paper and showed them to Mama.

"Look at this name," he said. "If this person could be brought into the business as a partner or into the family, he could pay for the slot for Ren-ren. You are an intelligent woman. Have you ever thought of this?"

Mama stared at the paper, not answering.

"At least the son has been allowed into your house," Fung said, removing his spectacles. "You may be getting your way with your husband at last."

She seemed calmer. "He refused to go and see the Honorable," she said. "Do you see how he pretended to get sick? Do you see how he pretended to get an attack of illness?"

"At least the son is coming," Fung insisted.

"Yes, he is coming," Mama admitted. "At least Papa has allowed that. He says that the sons are not responsible for the sins of their fathers."

I held my breath. There was more to Bingo's coming than I realized. I closed my eyes. He would be my knight in shining armor. He had been promised to me in all the books I'd read, in all the movies I'd seen.

Finally Mama simply shrugged. The money was gone. Arguing with Uncle Fung would not get it back. Perhaps his advice was good—wait and see what influence would do instead.

CHAPTER SIX

The following week, Bingo came, and life became interesting for me. It was rumored that Bingo had some Northern Chinese blood in his veins, since he was the son of the Honorable from the Honorable's second wife. Bingo had the aquiline nose and the high cheekbones of the men from Manchuria, a real *pak-la,* Mama said. They are sneaky, she said, you have to watch out for them.

I thought he would work in the dining room, where we could get better acquainted, but Papa assigned him to the kitchen basement, where his job was to pick celery and to grow bean sprouts. He also subbed as a short-order cook, helping Positive-Plus Uncle with the *chop-suey* stirrings in the wok-pot.

Bingo did not seem to mind these assignments. He said he preferred them to the snobbish ways of the dining room, which was really the domain of Uncle Fung anyway.

He was a very likable young man, happy with his hunks of celery, sitting on an old orange crate, talking to me, listening to old "wampum" tales of "Injun Joe", the garbage collector.

We got along well those first weeks. When he wasn't busy, we would go for walks at Fountain Lake Park, where he would show me how to fly a kite and swim. In the evenings, once a week he would take me dancing at the AF of L hall. He did everything effortlessly, as if it were a baseball game and he the lead pitcher. He called me "Cutie," which put me off base.

You can't imagine the change in my life. Before, there was Margie of the Twelves and the restaurant and Olley, the organ player and old Doc. Now there was appreciation and stimulation and no criticism from Big Mouth. She watched Bingo and me with approval, clucking and nodding, as if to say, "My dear, you are a little fat, but if you play your cards right, you may have a boyfriend."

I worshiped him. I would sit at his feet, nodding to his words, but really looking at his supple body, neat in a T-shirt open at the throat.

Sooner or later he would get on his favorite topic of conversation—the injustices of Americans to the Chinese. He told me about the Oriental Exclusion Acts, about racism in America, and how in past years Chinese couldn't become doctors or lawyers, that they had been forbidden by law to join these professions. I knew these facts because Papa was a great Chinese patriot also. But to tell you the truth, this talk bored me.

"All minorities in America get it in the neck," Bingo said. "The United States government passed laws that forced us to lie. They excluded Chinese, Japanese, and Filipinos. But poor people will always want to come to America if they can. Only when the Europeans came, it was okay. Discrimination starts being economic. Then it becomes racial."

"What do you mean?" (It seems I was always saying What do you mean?)

"You have to lie to survive. Once you have a paper name you don't know who you are. You become a liar."

I knew of what he spoke. Take Roy Lee and Yee Ting of Chicago, Bingo's two brothers. They all had different names, because they were the "paper sons" of two different people. But the whole process was bad because you had to bribe the immigration officials, bribe the consulate in Hong Kong—everything was a bribe.

I said petulantly, "Oh, I'm tired of hearing about our people. I know how we got to America. We were coolies and we built the railroads. Then they passed the Exclusion Acts, and we had to find devious ways of getting into this country. That was when the family associations invented the slot system—everybody's birth certificate gets lost in the San Francisco earthquake. What do you think Mama talks about all the time? When is Papa going to get a false paper for my cousin Ren-ren? That's all I hear, morning, noon, and night. It's sickening."

"That's because you're only half Chinese," Bingo said lightly.

"What do you mean, half Chinese?"

He never answered that question except with a smile. "Someday you will understand, Chingaling. Someday when you are older."

The "ho" used to be my favorite meeting spot. It meant "hole" and had been coined by Margie and her brash brothers for a gully by the railroad track behind their house, which was partly shaded by a large cottonwood tree. The M&St.L (Minneapolis and St. Louis Railroad) had left some empty oil drums in the area, and as children we loved to sit inside them and read Batman or Superman comics or *True Love Stories*. Sometimes we had to fight with tramps for the spot so we could learn how to smoke (it was better than being caught smoking in the barn).

Bingo walked me to the familiar spot under the cotton- wood. The oil drums had long since disappeared, but the "ho" was still private and cozy.

"Blindman's buff," Bingo said. "Close your eyes. I have a surprise for you." He put his hand into my hand and said "Feel." It was a box. "Now open your eyes when I count: one, two, three—yippee!"

It was the most beautiful pendant I had ever seen. In the sun, the jewels glistened. "Gold and jade," he explained, "the monad of the yin and yang, the Chinese way. It once belonged to my mother. I wanted to give it to a girl—someone I felt could use it. It's for you, from me."

"Me?" My heart jumped.

"Jade is for luck," he said very solemnly. "You are American and Chinese. The two cultures should be wedded in harmony."

"Do you mean it's mine for keeps?"

"For keeps." He laughed.

What did it mean? I was the kind of person who needed a diagram, a drawing and explanations with all the i's dotted and the t's crossed. But that was all he would say.

"Let's go for a walk," he added shortly.

We went to the viaduct, over Chicken Hill, which was the town's lover's lane. The hill surrounded Big Lake, which enclosed several small islands. In the summer you could paddle a canoe through the cove and go through a sea of weeping willows.

"Now it's your turn to make a wish," I said.

He laughed. "Wishes are for girls."

"Okay." I closed my eyes.

"What did you wish for?" he said.

"I wished that you would seal it with a kiss."

"That's an easy wish." He bent over and kissed me. It was the first time I had ever been kissed, a French kiss, even. Nicer than Margie had said, nicer than books had made possible. I jumped up. "Stop," I said.

He laughed. "Okay." He wiped his mouth. "Now make a real wish." I did.

"What did you wish now?"

"It's a secret."

What did I wish? What indeed, but that he would never leave me.

"What do you think of Helen, the Indian waitress?" I asked, two days later. We were sitting in his favorite lecture spot, the basement, on two crates next to a clump of ripening bananas.

"I think she's a real woman."

"What, do you mean by that? That I'm not a real woman?"

He kissed me behind the ear. "You're not dry yet behind your ears. But I hope you grow up to be a real woman."

"You know what I think she is," I said quickly. I whispered something in his ear.

"I can't hear you. Say it louder."

"I'll spell it: W_____."

"Oh, for Pete's sake," he said."You're jealous.

"That just goes to show you, that you're not grown up yet. You're a girl-woman." He spoke the words lightly, but I was angry.

"She flirts with everyone," I said. "And she's running around with Stormy Steene, the cab driver. I heard they neck every night at Lower Lake. She doesn't wear any underclothes."

"You should get to know her. She's very nice. Nice," he repeated.

"I haven't the slightest idea what you mean." My tone had a cutting edge. Was he hiding a secret from me? But he did not elaborate.

"Helen lives above a grocery store," I volunteered. "That's probably why she lives up there, so she can entertain men. I heard it was because of a man that she left Glenville and came to the Canton. The hotel wouldn't hire her, but you know Papa and his kind heart. He'd hire anybody because he feels sorry for them."

Bingo just looked at me and grinned, so I raised my voice.

"And she doesn't have a telephone," I said. "Once Papa tried to call her up to tell her to work the split shift one Saturday night, and she told him later that she didn't have a telephone. Why shouldn't a person want a telephone? What's she trying to hide?"

"You shouldn't listen to gossip," Bingo said.

He opened up two cans of beer and handed me one. "Do me a favor during your break," he said. "Go over to Skinner's and buy me six pairs of nylon stockings, size ten."

"Who are the stockings for? I bet they're for Helen. Well, that does it!" I yelled. "Here I help you pick celery for the *chop suey* and you ask me to buy stockings for her."

Laughing, he handed me twenty dollars.

"Oh, you make me mad!" I wailed. "You treat me like some kind of slave around here, like Papa sending me out to buy shorts for Positive-Plus Uncle because he can't speak English. Do you know how embarrassing that is?"

"Keep the change. Buy yourself something nice."

"Don't take any wooden nickels," I said. Actually I wanted to burst into tears.

That was the incident that made me decide to "get Bingo." It was not the scheme of a proper Chinese girl.

In our town, if a girl got "into trouble," there was a marriage, hastily arranged in Iowa (so the neighbors wouldn't know) and the date kept a dark secret. Then a church supper would be held a week later. "Post-nuptial gathering," it was called in the *Evening Tribune.*

I figured that with the proper preparations, Bingo would succumb. For the next weeks, therefore, I spent hours with all the books I could find on pregnancy at the public library. I mulled over temperature charts and kits. Ovulation was in my daily vocabulary. The only question was the timing. I had to get Bingo alone. It had to be soon or never.

It was a daring plan, and I never considered the consequences. Bingo had two rooms, one at the Hotel Majestic and one upstairs in our house. The upstairs bedroom was sometimes occupied by cooks who would come in during Mondays, when the restaurant was closed. In my inventive mind, I associated such visits with gambling and illicit traffic with women. I envisioned opium dens, taken from my readings about the Orient in American textbooks.

Bingo, however, was involved in more terrible things than mere opium. There were pictures of Communists like Mao Tze-tung hidden in his room and other Chinese readings I did not understand. His was, I feared, a more alien world that I wished to know about.

In the afternoon, I decided to go up to Fountain Lake Park and take a swim. I would practice the strokes that Bingo had taught me. In the park itself, about fifty feet from the beach, I saw two boys kicking a football. Near the gazebo, two children of Mr. Ommens, the bandleader, practiced twirling their batons. On the beach, some friends from high school waved. "Bingo's here," one of the girls said. "Boy, can he swim."

I looked in the direction of their fingers. I saw nothing but a lot of bathers near the viaduct. Maybe he will drown, I thought, and all my troubles will be over.

I lay back on a towel and tried to get a suntan. I took out a copy of *Modern Screen,* and pleasant reveries of Marlon Brando passed through my imagination. I shut my eyes but kept thinking of Bingo.

A moment later I saw him. He had come up to me and was looking down and grinning. His straight legs made me stare. He was not thin like most Chinese men but muscular in his thighs and arms. He took a towel and dried himself. Then he lighted a cigarette and sat down.

"Still mad?" he said.

"No."

"May I sit down?"

"If you want to. Do as you like. It's a free country."

"I want to say that I admire you, Chingaling. But sometimes you have to think before you act." He extended his hand. "Friends?" he said.

"Friends."

He smiled. "Let's go for a swim. Show me how much you've learned."

"Where do you want to go?"

"To the viaduct," he said. "I'll tow you out."

"Oh, okay."

He took my hand, and together we went into the lake. I relaxed in the comfort of his expert swimming. The sky was heavy with clouds, and you could smell the scent of dying blossoms and hear the wind in the bushes. When we got back, I dried my hair and sniffed the air and listened to his portable radio.

"You're not a little girl anymore," he said.

"Size eleven," I said proudly. "I'm bigger across the chest than most Chinese girls." I leaned forward to demonstrate.

He laughed. "Why don't you give me a cousinly kiss?"

I shook my head.

"What's the matter?"

What was I supposed to say? How could I tell him I wanted him to liberate me from the house, from Mama and Papa, from the restaurant, from this town? "Bingo," I shouted, "I love you."

For a moment he stared at me in disbelief. He didn't say anything for a minute.

"But I do love you," I insisted.

"You're not serious?"

"Yes. I'd like to know what it's like."

"No," he said. "I couldn't."

"Don't you find me attractive?"

"It has nothing to do with that, Chingaling. It would be too great a burden on me. I can't take that kind of responsibility."

"But I want it. It's got to happen sometime."

"Yes. But not with me."

"Why not?"

"Because you're too emotional. You're too impulsive. Because you're not grown up yet. Because of a lot of reasons that I can't explain to you because you're still a child."

"I ask you something and you give me a sermon." He wasn't pulling any wool over my eyes. He didn't like me—that was obvious.

After a long pause, he said carefully, "Of course, that would be how you would interpret everything. Black and white. Because that's the way you want to see it. Look, if I say cut it out now, you will needle me to stick a pin in me. I won't let you do that."

Was this love, this awful feeling in the pit of my stomach?

He lighted a cigarette and puffed several times, as if he must choose his words carefully. "You've been awfully good to me this summer, Chingaling," he said.

I didn't answer. I dropped my eyes down to the blanket and looked at some of the bathers. I seemed to have forgotten all reason.

Bingo put his arms around my shoulders and drew me close to him. "Next year at this time, you'll have lots of boyfriends, and you'll be laughing at all of this."

"No," I murmured, "never."

He tried to tell me a joke to make me laugh. But I didn't feel like laughing.

In the park the boys were hitting a ball aimlessly across the field. Some girls in shorts darted after them. Bingo was smoking carefully and looking out beyond the trees.

"I plan to go back to China."

"So what's the big deal?"

"Mainland China. I would have to live on a commune. Life is very regimented there."

What was he trying to say? I didn't get the point. He began to talk. "I have seen men sick with opium because of the absentee-landlord system in China that existed before Mao Tze-tung came into power. Do you know that in Shanghai there was so much starvation that burial crews had to come to take the bodies off the streets?"

China, Shmima—he could be talking about darkest Africa. How could I know these things? I had only lived in Minnesota.

"You know," I said, "somebody could report you to the State Department."

"What I'm trying to say is that I can't do anything about you because my life is tied up with the Movement. I can't expect you to understand this because you've spent all your life here; you think American."

"There you go again, about thinking American. How can I think American when morning, noon, and night Papa tells me I'm Chinese?"

He smiled. "You will understand when you get older, when you are more mature. This society is already formed. Its people have enough to eat, its population is educated. China is a society being formed again, you might say. In a hundred years, if we don't get in a war, it may be like America. But then we would have to meet again in another life."

He was crazy. He was one of those crazy Communist students that Auntie Tong has warned me about. She told me that up at the university they were at Farm Campus, lounging around in wrinkled blue suits and getting up in the morning and dancing the *yang-ko*. All of them belonged to that Communist front organization, the Chinese Student Christian Association. I could not listen to any more of the conversation. This was a subject I did not understand or want to understand. It was better when he talked about the old days of the tong wars. That was past. But he was talking about a future that did not include me.

"I certainly am more honest than you," I said. "At least I admit what I want. I'm no hypocrite."

He made a futile gesture. "What's the use?" he said. 'You're just a child."

"You said it again. Why?"

"Because you interpret everything I say in the way you want to hear it."

"Oh, here we go again," I said. "All my faults and none of yours."

"Come on, Chingaling, let's change the subject."

"Why don't you go and talk to Helen , that Indian?" I said to him.

"Perhaps I will."

He gathered his clothes and walked away. I started after him and then turned around and went back to the beach. I waited, hoping he would come running back, but I saw that he was already in the park.

The following morning Bingo tried to make amends. He was sitting in the waitress booth behind the soda fountain. Acutely embarrassed, I went to the back of the door without a word, took down a busboy jacket, put it on, and began making syrup for the teenage soda trade.

"Hey, Chingaling," Bingo said gently. "How about bringing me a setup?"

I gave him a look of annoyance, but brought him a tray of club soda and ice cubes.

"Thanks," Bingo said.

Then he bent over and purred at the back of my neck. "You're sweet."

"The sweetest," I said haughtily.

He ignored this and went over and put a quarter in the jukebox.

"Come on," he said, "let's dance."

"How come you like to play fan-tan so much?" I said, relenting a bit.

He shrugged his shoulders. "It's relaxing."

"I don't understand you," I said. "You're in law school. You're going to make something of yourself. But you spend so much time playing fan-tan."

"It's cultural," he teased. "Get two Chinamen together, and you have a fan-tan game."

"There's nothing wrong with being professional," I said. "Don't you want people to be proud of you?"

He shrugged his shoulders. "Those college engineers at the university bore me. And the ones from Taiwan." He made a face. "All they talk about is the servants they have and the chauffeurs. All on American money given overseas." He was pensive. "That's why Mayor Johnny is right. We have got to lobby in Congress to change the immigration laws. In ten years things will start to change. In the meantime, it's fan-tan for me."

"You refuse to compete."

"I've got habits, honey, and it's hard to change them."

"You ought to visit the university more often," I said.

"You could meet Chinese in the fraternities. The Alpha Lambda and the FF."

His answer was a swear.

Oh, I was furious. "Do you have to swear?"

"Damn it," he said. "You're not even in college yet, and you know what Chinese fraternities they have."

"What are you talking about?"

"I'll tell you what I'm talking about. I'm talking about justice and what it's all about. You take poor Ben or Lim or half a dozen other people. Sure, they're in here illegally. But the immigration guys get down on them—shakedowns. You'd think they'd stolen a million dollars. Your Chinese shakedown artists get down on them. That's why the association has to be strong. You think we planned it this way? We didn't. But that's how you survive in this culture." He took a swig of whiskey. "In ten years things will be different. In the meantime, here's to gambling."

"That's an excuse," I said. "You like being with crooks." I tried to give him a stern look by raising my eyebrows. "Can you tell me what you enjoy about being with a bunch of gamblers who can hardly speak English?" There it was back, the feeling of loneliness that haunted me had returned in monstrous shape. I looked at him defiantly.

"I can't explain it to you," he said. "To me, they're real guys. And they're simple, like me."

I gave no sign of hearing him. "A lot of them play around with the waitresses," I said. "And they get them pregnant."

He gave me a sad look.

"They have no sense of responsibility," I continued. "They have wives in China, wives all over the place, but they don't care what they do, whom they play around with, whom they hurt. .

"Honey, you look much better when you're smiling," Bingo said.

"If only they had a sense of responsibility," I continued. "It hurts all of us—."

"Hey, when winter comes, I'll take you skiing in the lake country," he interrupted.

"A lot of time could be saved if people didn't waste their time on frivolous things and set their minds on what was really important in life. After all, you have only one life to live."

Bingo was now laughing furiously.

"You can't take anything seriously," I shouted. "Go back to China! Go to your Indian girl friend. We just don't communicate."

CHAPTER SEVEN

It was Saturday night. The town was dry because of the power of the Women's Christian Temperance Union. On Saturday nights, everyone got a bottle and came to the restaurant after midnight to whoop it up. There was usually a fistfight around one o'clock and Papa would call Big Karl, who always arrived after the fighting parties had made up and were singing "Sweet Adeline" in the men's room. It became a Canton routine—as much a part of life as the raising of the American flag, rain or shine.

At about nine o'clock, the seven o'clock show was over at the Bijou, and the customers for hot pork tenderloin sandwiches and a plate of *chow mein* began to pour in. There was a lot of mixing between booths and a lot of swearing. At eleven the first fistfight took place. One of the guys from Mud Jens's baseball club punched one of the Swenson gang in the jaw. Papa broke it up by telling them they had to sit down and eat or he was going to call the cops. Then the plumbing in the ladies room got stopped up.

We were busy filling Baby, the bus cart with whiskey smuggled in from Austin, which we got from the union hall. Ray, the silverware salesman, came in with free samples of napkin rings and cake cutters. Mayor Johnny showed up after midnight with three giggling women with animal heads wrapped around their necks. I recognized the ladies as three of Johnny's regular Palm Garden companions. Old Doc loitered around reading the *Evening Tribune* and clipping out items in the local news columns.

"Sam, you got a good crowd out tonight," Johnny greeted Papa, as he taxied his Palm Garden ladies in front of him. "If you have any trouble, you know Big Karl's number at the police station."

One of the ladies giggled and reached into the restaurant cart. She uncorked a whiskey bottle and took a sip.

"Hey, the union is watering down the stuff. Sammy, how about some setups?"

"Hope you have a good time tonight," Papa said. "Don't do nothing I wouldn't do now."

Johnny gave me a quarter to put in the jukebox. I played a Frank Sinatra number.

By the time Olley the organ player joined them, everybody was high. But they got annoyed when he wouldn't take off his hat.

"Where do you think you are?" one Palm Garden lady said. "This is Sammy's. It ain't church."

Johnny told the lady to pipe down. He gave Olley a shot in a glass with some ice. "Settle yourself and have some pepper-upper. Is the current picture worth seeing?"

"It's no *Gone with the Wind*," Olley said. Then, "Johnny, I gotta talk to you. I got ESP. I have a feeling this is going to be our last celebration at the Canton."

"What do you mean?" Johnny said. "The lease is certain to be renewed. Mr. Sorensen has always come through."

"I'm not talking about the lease, Johnny; I'm talking about competition. Do you know Dea, who owns the taxicabs in town? He's putting up a steak house right on Highway Sixteen. What do you think of that? When Sam was so good to Dea. Let him use the telephones, let his boys call in and get their orders. All free of charge."

Johnny blinked. He was a little rattled. "Well," he said thoughtfully, "I'd sure like to know what your source of information is."

Olley called over Ray, the silverware salesman. "Ray knows all about it. He sold Dea some restaurant supplies last week, didn't you, Ray?"

The group stared malevolently at Ray. Ray just shrugged his shoulders. "It's true," he said. "But competition never hurts no one."

"Dea has a funny sense of humor," Johnny acknowledged, obviously understanding the point Olley was making. "Still, Ray is right. Competition never hurt no one. And the Canton still has the best steaks in town."

"It's dog eat dog," Olley said. "Do you know what's going to happen to all of us if we don't have the Canton to come to anymore. Where are we going to go? Sammy's a gentleman. You don't have many gentlemen left these days. You chew on that for a minute." They chewed. Somehow the thinking made everyone morose. Nobody wanted any more pepper-upper.

"Hey, let's go over to the Palm Garden," one of the ladies said, tugging at Johnny's arm. "The Canton is dead."

I could not concentrate on my work. Ordinarily, I enjoyed Saturday nights. When business slowed down, I went down to the basement looking for Bingo to fix me up a pork tenderloin sandwich. But tonight he wasn't there. Papa told me that he was in his room at our house. I called home. There was no answer.

As we got ready to close up, Uncle Fung said, "Something bothering you, Fat."

"No," I lied.

"Why don't you go home?" he suggested. "Your ma and dad and I can clean up."

Papa waved me over. "If you are going home, go wake up Helen," he said. "Tell her I want her to work the split shift tomorrow. Tell her Big Mouth sick and can't make it. Maybe she forget. I don't want her forget."

"Papa, I wish you'd tell her to get a phone," I said.

"Tell her I want to take Toastmasters tomorrow," he hollered at me in English. "Mayor Johnny coming for dinner."

Charlie Stevens, the town drunk, was hauled away to jail by Big Karl, leaving a plate of *chow mein* half eaten. Unannounced, Ray, the silverware salesman, handed out a bunch of chances for an automobile, collecting a buck apiece from anyone still around. Papa cleaned the mirrors with ammonia and swished the floor with soap and water. I filled the sugar bowls and the napkin holders, and emptied the Baby, the bus cart. I was tired, but not from overwork. Thirsty, I drank three Cokes and ate two hamburgers. I wanted to get away from it all—all the dreary rooms and the straight-backed chairs and calendars from the milk company.

Helen lived on the second floor of a grocery store. I ran up the stairs and pounded at the door.

"You make sure to come to work tomorrow," I shouted. "All the Toastmasters are coming in, and Papa doesn't have enough help."

I heard a giggle. "Who is it? Is that you, Ching?" she said. She came to the door, wrapped in a shawl, looking sleepy.

Her face looked pale. Its keen features and high cheekbones gave her the air of a young princess. But what drew my eyes was her neck. For there it was—exactly the same jade heart that Bingo had given to me.

In the recesses of my mind I had been betrayed. Like the blind man touching the elephant, I ran down the stairs whispering "traitor" at her and at him. He had seen her and beckoned and she had run. How could he compare me (a person of my high stature) to *her?*

The streets were dark, but I ran as if carrying a torch to light my way. When I got home, I was exhausted. I sat on my bed and began to eat. Peanuts, candy, anything within sight.

After a while, I washed my face. Then I wandered upstairs to Bingo's room and knocked on the door. "Bingo," I whispered. "Are you there?"

There wasn't any answer. He had probably gotten dressed and gone out—leaving the lights on. I went in. His pants were flung carelessly over a chair, and there were many books on the windowsill. I fingered a kewpie doll that he had won at the county fair and a "Good Night, Sweetheart" United States Marines pillow.

Where was he? I went outside in the yard and sniffed the night air. There was the scent of roses in the yard. I spent the next hour thinking and thinking about Helen and the jade heart.

He had been with her in her room. She would get pregnant and he would have to marry her.

I walked like a cat into the kitchen. The cleaver stood gleaming in the stump. I had wondered all summer what I needed, what I wanted. And there it was. I picked it up and walked upstairs to

Bingo's rooms and waited alone. I shivered, for I could not stop the beating of my heart.

I did not have to wait long. He came whistling up the stairs. Why didn't he go back to the hotel? I thought. It's because he's been with her. He wants to show off. How dare he come to our house when he's been with her?

He turned on the light. "Hi, Ching," he said. "Something wrong?"

I was sitting on his bed. I had the knife behind my back. Desolate, I revealed its blade, shaking it before him like a fist.

"I'm going to kill you," I said. "Tonight you are going to die."

If he laughs, I won't let him count to ten, I thought. But he did nothing at all. I just stood before him shaking the knife.

"You gave that Indian a jade just like mine, didn't you?" I said. "And all that talk you gave me that it was special! You wanted me to remember you. For what?"

"Chingaling, let me explain."

I backed away, still holding the knife. "I mean it," I said. "You keep away from me."

"Chingaling, you're too emotional, too impulsive."

"Go ahead, call me names. I'm not afraid of you. But say something," I hollered. "Say something."

He stared at me.

"If you don't like me, why did you give me the jade heart?"

He shook his head. "Because I wanted to. Because I do like you. Because I wanted to give it to you as a friendship present to remind you of me."

I couldn't stand it. He wanted friendship. He treated me like Margie of the Twelves. I could only interpret it in that way. I had offered him my body, and he had refused. He had humiliated me beyond repair.

"Why do you hurt yourself so, Chingaling?" he said finally. His voice was tender, yet eager. I looked at his fine features, the thin, taut face with those high cheekbones. The knife fell to the floor.

"God, what's the matter with you?" he said soothingly. "Why do you need so much affection?"

"I don't want to be Chinese," I sobbed. "I want to be American!"

He took me in his arms. "It's okay," he said. "It's okay."

For a long time we just kissed. Then his hand slid up and down my neck. He kissed my throat and my neck.

"Bingo, I want to go all the way," I said.

"Do you mean it?"

"Yes."

At that moment, we heard the door slam.

"Are you home from the restaurant?" I heard Mama call out. "Don't waste electricity."

Panic-stricken, I leaped away from him.

"It's all right," he said. "Just be quiet."

"No," I whispered back. "Tomorrow, tomorrow at three o'clock. Mama always goes to the restaurant to get her Chinese mail. Then Auntie Tong visits and they compare children. And she will be gone for hours."

We broke apart, and I sneaked in the dark to my room.

Exhilarated, I stretched out on my bed. I hugged myself. How could I justify this hunger for him? Suddenly, I leaped out of bed and rushed to my table, where I kept bottles of cologne and lipsticks and makeup. I rouged my cheeks and painted my eyes.

I felt I had him within my grasp at last. I felt like a young bride, ready to sever the umbilical cord to her parents, ready to cut the hated hymen.

"You should pray," Big Mouth had said. "God answers your prayers." So during the night I prayed.

"Dear God. I won't ask anything again. Just make him love me. Make me pregnant. Then make him marry me."

That was the extent of my belief. Since I never attended Sunday school except sporadically to please the mission ladies, I believed that God could be summoned at will. It was an act of respect, like signing a petition to get a star on your spelling book.

The next morning dawned bright and clear. Would he remember? I wondered. I watched the sun rise up over the grain elevator. I got dressed and didn't wear a brassiere. I figured that would make me sexier.

It was three o'clock. The events progressed exactly as I had planned. Frightened and a little guilty, I hid behind a fir tree in the neighbor's yard until I saw Mama slam the porch door and go out, her hair tied up in a head scarf, carrying her black pocketbook over her arm, her stockings halfway rolled up above her ankles. She looked like a person from a strange planet who was very much at home. I ran upstairs to Bingo's room. Breathless, I knocked.

"Hi, Chingaling," he said quietly. "I saw your mother go out. Are you sure this is what you want?"

Couldn't he read my mind? My heart was ticking; I could feel the pain beneath my stomach. What do you think? I thought. Can't you believe I have been living for this moment?

I sat down on his bed. We kissed. He undid his shirt. I strained against him.

I gasped at his slim body in broad daylight. It was like quicksilver lightning, a thin warrior's sword. He was my samurai—or was that Japanese? I didn't care, but began flinging off my shirt. As usual my hands were flabby, I couldn't get to the buttons. Would he think me terribly fat? Obviously not; he was kissing my neck, my hair, and muttering in a sort of eager whisper.

"I can't get this button."

"Here, let me help you."

Then we heard a noise.

What was that? Oh, my goodness! It was Mama! "She's home early," I whispered, aghast. "Something must have happened."

He had leaped up and stood before me. I heard a door slam.

"Mama, is that you?" I called to her from the top of the stairs.

I heard a moan—then something like "Ching, help me." Then the door slammed again.

"It's Mama," I told Bingo. "She's gone crazy. Something has happened."

I ran down the stairs, Bingo following, putting on his shirt on the way.

"The garden," said Bingo. "Auntie Wing must be in the garden."

Of course, where else? If not kissing the ancestral goddess, Kwan Yin, if not in the bedroom with her letters and her memories of Toy San, then she must be in the garden, where she planted her vegetables.

We rushed into the backyard, to Mama's beloved garden with the bitter melon, the *fu-ga* vines, the *vooh,* or Chinese potatoes. There we found her, sitting among the vegetables, her eyes looking into space.

"Mama, Mama."

She did not speak. She just swayed back and forth and moaned in a strange, high-pitched key. She had a letter in her hand, and Ren-ren's picture was in her lap. "He's gone," she could only say. "Cholera. He's gone."

Papa. I had to call Papa. After all, he was Mama's husband, the head of the family.

"Don't call your father," she shrieked suddenly. "It's all his fault. He is so slow about doing anything." Mama had gone crazy. An odd moan came like the wind across from China, her homeland. "He did it," she screamed. "It's all his fault. He was the one who put me in this jail."

"It's all right, Auntie Wing, it's all right," Bingo said to her. He stroked her hair, and she began to respond and whimper.

But what about me? I wondered. What about me?

He seemed to know that some terror had hit my mother, and I was more interested in myself. There was something forbidden in the look that then passed between Bingo and me. I knew then and there that his need for me would never make itself known again.

Half an hour later Bingo arrived with Dr. Kemp, who carried a little brown-green bag from which he took a needle.

"She won't take a needle," I told the doctor. "She won't."

"Give her these pills five times a day, then," Dr. Kemp said. "It will help her to sleep."

"She won't take them. She says she won't take anything. She wants to remember him."

The doctor shook his head. "Tell her that she needs some sleep. Tell her that in Chinese."

Papa did not come the next day or the next. Mama stayed in her room, the door locked. By the fifth day, we were able to get her to take the pills. Bingo would come and knock on her door and sort of force them down her. I wondered, watching him, if he had been used to grief.

"Papa wasn't here when she needed him," I told Bingo. "What a coward."

Bingo said nothing. "Well, sometimes your parents let you down," he said. "Even the best of them."

"Would you talk to him? I can't."

"No, it's none of my business. I am not of the same family. I cannot interfere in matters that don't concern me."

"How come Papa won't come to her?" I asked him. When he didn't answer, I said, "He's her husband. He should have been there when the doctor came. He ran away. That's what he did. He ran away."

It was the last day in July. As I prepared to get ready to work the night shift, I realized how much our family had become dependent on Bingo. It suddenly occurred to me that if he ever stepped out of our lives, we might fall apart. The thought was very sobering and terrible.

Big Mouth was the only one who made any reference to the state of affairs at home.

"You've got to get her to talk about it," she would advise me. "Otherwise she's going to hold it against Sammy. And Sammy needs all the moral support he can get right now."

"How come my father stayed away then?" I demanded.

When she didn't answer, I said, "He's her husband. He should have been there when the doctor came. He stayed away. That's what he did. He stayed away. He's a big coward."

"Your father has enough on his mind. After all, you can't expect your father to know everything."

Big Mouth said, "You're their child. It's up to you to take care of both of them. Your dad keeps everything inside. So you've got to be the person each one talks to. You don't want both of them to go nuts, do you?"

I could not answer that question. I was glad the summer was coming to a close. I did not want their problems on my shoulders. Their lives were practically over, I figured. Mine was just beginning.

"Your father worries about your ma," Big Mouth said.

"Sammy worries about both of you. But he has a lot on his mind. Boy, I wish Mr. Sorensen would get here and renew the lease."

In August, the town prepared for fall. Olsen's Department store changed its picture window and took the white shoes off the lady dummies. Wallace's showed Back to School fashions.

At the Palm Garden, they began serving whiskey out in the open—a test case, as Mayor Johnny put it. "Freedom someday will prevail."

Papa ordered a new American flag for the restaurant and a red-white-and-blue awning. The Bird Watchers Society sent out notices to watch for the flight of birds south, and the Ladies' Christian Temperance Union met for tea at the home of Mrs. Olaf Lundgren. According to rumor (Big Mouth's gossip) they made popcorn, denounced the Catholics and began a new quilt for the DAR. They also denounced the editor of neighboring Freeborn County's biggest newspaper, a member of Who's Who in American Women and a pacifist. But she was also a DAR and had known Sinclair Lewis when he taught up at the university. The latest gossip was that she must have been a Socialist in those days.

Afternoons in the restaurant were lazy hours. Although the schoolteachers had returned from summer vacation, most didn't come in to eat until around six o'clock, so I had a lot of spare time to look at movie magazines and draw ladies' legs. Mama's moods had moved from low to periods of high vitality. She would get housekeeping spurts and start cleaning up shelves and washing dishes a couple of times.

A month passed. No sign of Mr. Sorensen. Already the "Welcome Home, Honorable Restaurant Landlord" streamer over the Coca-Cola sign looked droopy. The red lanterns were returned to the Wing Laundry Association in Chicago.

Finally Fung gave the word to take the sign down. I could tell he was worried. He didn't talk about Houston anymore.

Big Mouth saw it first (it was hardly noticed in the *Tribune*, since it was in "local news"). Even Olley was outscooped.

I. Sorensen Announces Sale of Building on Main Street. Filling-station interest may buy building and raze the premises . . . plan to open Phillips 66 franchise . . . All current leases expire at the end of the month . . . The longest lease is that held by the Canton Café.

"Oh, jeepers!" Big Mouth cried. "What's Sammy going to do?"

As usual, Papa did nothing. He sat in the back booth, still as death, and drummed his fingers on the table and looked up at the sky. He began eating a day-old doughnut and threw it away in the trash can after two bites. He only made me promise that I wouldn't tell Mama.

"She has enough trouble already," he said quietly. "I know you think your Mama's stupid because she never read any books. But never think that, daughter, never think that."

It was terrible the following week, after we got the eviction notice. Every day, Papa went to the restaurant as if nothing had happened, as if the routine had not changed. Then he wiped the counter top so hard you thought the polish would wear away. After a long pause he would look at the embroidered silk peacock panels and the window with the air-conditioning sign "It's Cool Inside." His eyes got watery as if he couldn't see.

Finally, he would sit down in the back booth, call for a waitress, and order some fish. That was Papa, eating food that wasn't good for him. He had asthma, and Dr. Gable said that eating fish gave it to him. But Dr. Gable had died a year ago, and now Papa said he just had to visit the Mayo Clinic once a year to keep his health up. If he wanted to eat fish, that was his business. After spitting out the bones, he would go and visit with the customers and talk about the American Legion and the Chinese people.

Money, I thought. It always got down to money. There was no money for me to go to college now. There was no money to buy the building from Mr. Sorensen. Bingo came to me.

"Why don't you tell your ma?" he said. "She has a right to know."

"Why don't you tell her?"

"She's your ma, Ching. It's about time you started to grow up."

"She'll kill me. You know they never talk to their kids about what's important. You know, they're not like American parents."

In the end I told her. I can't tell you why I did, but I suppose it was to get even with Bingo. He said it was about time I started doing things that were right instead of things that were easy. I hated him so much that I told her. I told her that we had to get out of town while the getting was good. I told her we might go on relief. I told her that I would never marry a Chinese who had a restaurant.

She was quiet for a long, longtime. Well, I told her, just as he said, I thought. And it did no good, no good at all. "I guess that's the end of the family," I said.

"What did you say?"

"I said that's the end of the family."

She put on a kerchief.

"Where are you going, Ma?" I said.

"To the restaurant."

After a while, I decided I'd better go also.

When I got to the restaurant, I realized something had happened. Big Mouth was running back and forth with nothing in her hand, not even a towel, and Helen wasn't swishing her hips, and Uncle Fung was noncommittal. All three of them pointed to the back booth when I asked them where I could find Mama.

In the back booth, the canopy was closed. Within ten feet, I could hear Mama's shrill Cantonese dialect.

"You can talk about your Chinese history and your foreign devils and the imperialism which I don't understand," she was saying. "But I know only one thing. Mr. Sorensen did not renew the lease. You have no business. You cannot trust the *lo-fan*. You can only trust your own people, the Chinese. So you have your pride, so you have your family name. So you do not like gambling and opium, the world of China. There is that world in the United States too. It is just that you have been in this town too long to find out. But this time, I will have my way. This time you will not say no."

I heard Papa sigh. "They matched me up with a crazy woman," I heard him repeat. "In the village back home they matched me up with a crazy woman."

"We will use a go-between," she said then, "to speak to the Honorable. But after all these years, your silence with him must come to an end."

By that time, everyone was covering the back booth: Fung and Positive-Plus Uncle, Big Mouth, and Mayor Johnny with one of his Palm Garden ladies. "She looks sick," I said.

"Your mother's not sick," Johnny replied. "She's a strong little lady, and she has a lot of gumption. But she's not sick."

"Wife. . . ." Papa was saying.

"No, you will not interrupt. Oh, I know I am the nagger you say, but your silence is as bad as interruption. You have been in Gim-San over twenty years. You can't go to China because you hate the Communists, and you are too accustomed to life in this country. So we must make our bed where we lie.

"But you will not have to lose face. The meeting will be arranged through a go-between, an Ong, a member of my family. It will be in Chicago's Chinatown on Cermak Road. It will be done according to the custom in the village.

And you will have clean hands and a clean offer from the Honorable."

"What's happening?" Big Mouth interrupted.

"Mama, are you all right?" I asked her.

"Why don't you go and get some food for everybody," Mama said. "It's impolite for people to stand around and not have enough food in their stomachs."

CHAPTER EIGHT

Anyone who leaves our town takes the train from the Rock Island station. There is the Milwaukee station down the block, but that is just used for freight and for Old Man Anderson, who sits in the little house, eats from a box lunch, and flags down a couple of trains every so often. When it really comes to leaving town, you always take off from the Rock Island.

I thought about that on my last day home before going up to the university to school. As always, before I went on any trip, Mama had shown her love for me by cooking the food that I liked best. There were rice patties. There was *tung,* a rolled patty stuffed with walnuts and mushrooms and wrapped in banana leaves before steaming.

"Well," she said, greeting me in the kitchen as I brought my suitcase out. "The college girl. As usual, your Papa shows how much he loves you, sending you to college." She rolled a wonton patty.

"I suppose you haven't decided what you're going to study at the university."

"Journalism, Mama."

"What is this journalism?"

"It's writing for newspapers. Maybe I can come back and write for Old Man Sorensen," I joked.

The Rock Island station looked puny in the fall sunlight. Give it a few more years, I thought, and it'll sink into the snow. Out of habit, I set my bags down by the pushcarts and took a stroll between the tracks, jumping between the ties. Then a black car came up. From the driver's seat stepped Bingo.

Reluctantly, I went up to meet him.

I had wished that he would not come. It awakened the old longings in my heart, seeing Bingo here at the station.

"Back to the books," he said after I nodded at his greeting.

"Yes," I said.

"What did your father say?"

"Nothing much. Just told me to study hard and to make a list of what I needed."

"That's your dad," he said. "You have to read between the lines."

"Better late than never." I tried to laugh.

Papa had been given a share in a restaurant in San Francisco owned by the Honorable's brother. The Honorable said it was a union of two family associations in a business venture that would bring only good to both. Papa was to manage the restaurant. Knowing Papa, I assumed that it probably wouldn't make any money or bring any new shares into the Honorable's holdings, but it meant Papa could sit for hours and read his Chinese newspaper and tell the customers about Dr. Sun Yat-sen and Chiang Kai-shek. There wouldn't be any gambling in that restaurant, that's for sure. But that was Papa.

One of the trainmen came out of the station and waved to Bingo. "The Rocket will be on time," he said. Bingo nodded and went back to his car. He pulled out a long white package. "A present for me?" I said, trying to be calm.

"Roses," he said. "You always said you liked them."

Six long-stemmed roses, almost too cumbersome to carry.

"They'll wilt by the time I get to Minneapolis," I said.

"No. They are packed in ice."

We lapsed in silence. He didn't mention Mama or Papa or his father or the associations.

"Do you think Papa will ever go back to China?" I said instead.

Bingo said he didn't know. "I think it's an illusion," he said.

"You like my dad a lot, don't you?" I said.

"I like your whole family."

"I think your dad's a lot smarter. He certainly is richer."

"They are the same."

"What do you mean? My dad wears a busboy jacket, and he worships the Americans."

"They are the last of a generation, Ching. We won't see their likes again in America. They are dying out."

"Do you know how your father came over?" he said suddenly.

"How all of us came over? How I came over?"

He waited. "You were born here. You won't have that problem. When I go back, I plan to use my real name."

How Papa came over. Buying *chee*. Fraud. Lying. Everyone. Even Bingo. Paper son. He was a paper son. Papa—is that what Papa was afraid of? Is that what Papa was atoning for? His being a paper son, long ago?

"But not all Americans are bad," I said.

He shook his head. "I never said that. You are American. But don't forget you are also Chinese."

"That has nothing to do with us," I said quickly. "Why can't we get married? We could at least go steady. Or become engaged."

"I can't give myself to any girl now, Chingaling. My life is the movement of China."

A few weeks ago, I would have flown into a rage and shouted, "No, it's because of Helen. You love her!" But now I knew that he didn't love Helen any more than he loved me. I knew that he was serious about returning to China to live on a commune. And I was silent.

"You are going through some changes, too," he went on. "Just like I am. "He paused. "Haven't you ever done something impulsive that you feel sorry for later on?"

And then it dawned on me. He knew my secret. He knew about my writing graffiti on the walls. Stunned, I waited, but he did not elaborate. When I caught his eye, I knew: He wouldn't snitch on me any more than he would snitch on Helen. Had his mother really owned my jade heart? Maybe not, but he'd said that to make me feel good.

"You are Chinese," he said softly, "but mostly American."

"I think that's good," I said. "It's crazy to stay Chinese in Minnesota."

He did not reply. I knew that he was thinking of his home in China.

"Why do you have to go back?" I said suddenly.

"Some day, Ching," he said, "*you* will know why. " And we left it at that.

CPSIA information can be obtained at www.ICGtesting.com
Printed in the USA
BVOW08s1104270916

463408BV00001B/37/P

9 780738 817316